Dear Dawn,

Thank you

through the yec

enjoy this stor

Yours truly,

Also by H. W. Vivian

War of Rain
The Goddess: A War of Rain Novel
Chasers

Somewhere Beneath

A War of Rain Novel

H.W. Vivian

ISBN: 978-1-4834-6874-7 (sc)
ISBN: 978-1-4834-6873-0 (e)

Lulu Publishing Services rev. date: 04/24/2017

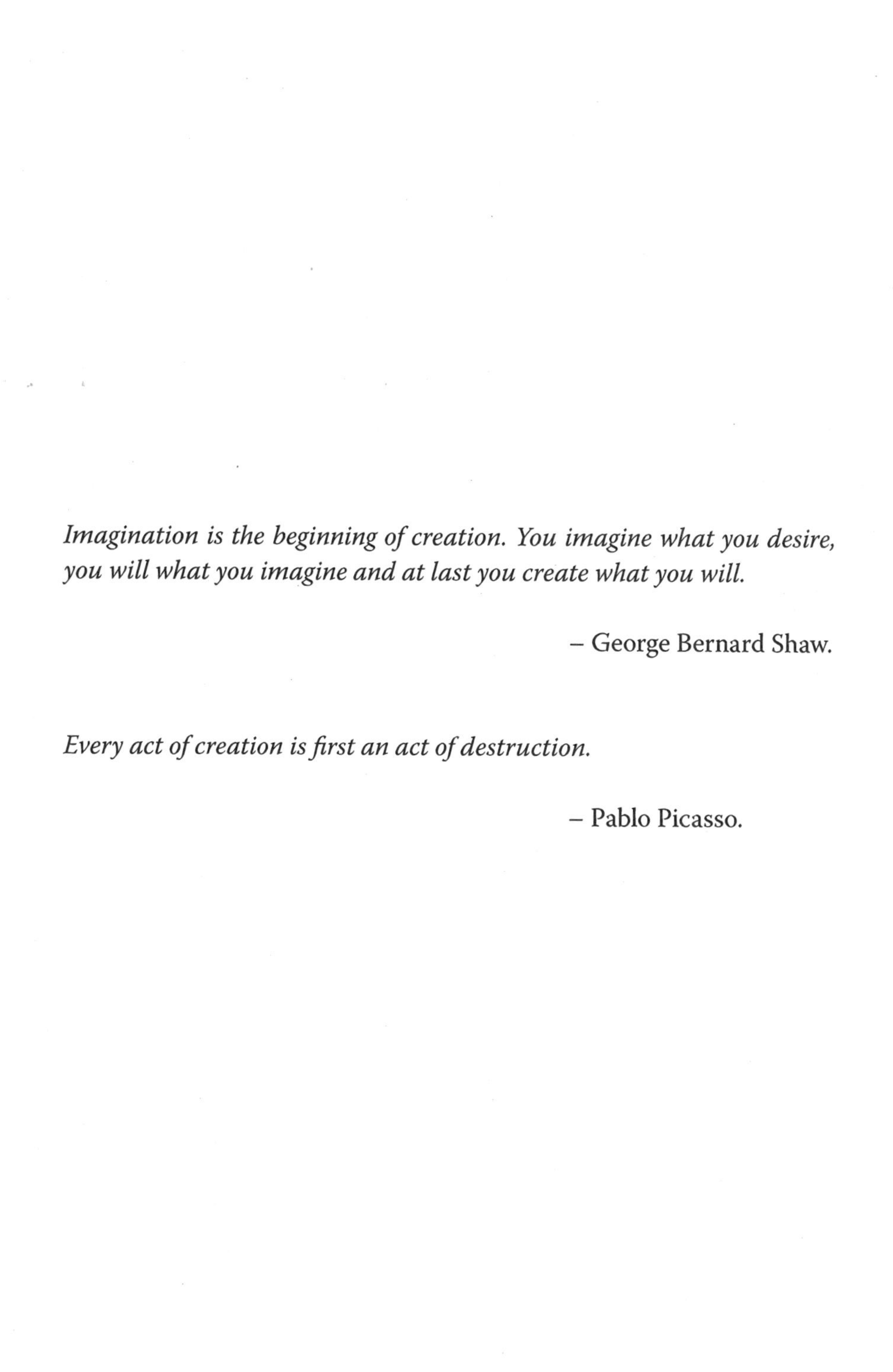

Imagination is the beginning of creation. You imagine what you desire, you will what you imagine and at last you create what you will.

– George Bernard Shaw.

Every act of creation is first an act of destruction.

– Pablo Picasso.

PROLOGUE

People of the past used to think that amazing inventions lay in the future—that there would be machines to help us think better, learn quicker, and understand everything down to its very molecular composition. My name is Alan, and I'm supposed to pioneer that future. The settlement I created is a giant metropolis called Terra-Mar, which exists beneath the earth's vast and endless ocean. Its glass enclosure sits on a network of metal grids to prevent it from breaking under the pressure of the sea floor.

My teacher tells me that many centuries ago, humanity fell from the stars in brilliant aircrafts of gems and light, landing in the very place they sought to escape from centuries earlier—the oceans of Earth. They endured impossible hardships—the rapid depletion of oxygen, the volatile water currents, the eventual deterioration of communication equipment. But eventually they regrouped and combined their efforts toward building one all-encompassing structure. Inside it, they became a small and secluded community, using the few advanced tools that survived the plummet from Mars.

Eleven years ago, when I was six, I first discovered my ability to create, and I used that ability to expand Terra-Mar into the prospering metropolis it is today.

I wake this morning in a twin-sized spring mattress set upon a metallic frame of my own design, the fluorescent light bulbs above activating with my movement. I squint toward the digital clock on a table near the opposite wall. The glowing red numbers reflect onto the dusty baseball that sits next to it. It's 09:10.

I was supposed to be in the lab ten minutes ago, I think worriedly. *Why didn't anyone wake me up?*

I close my eyes and strain my ears, waiting to hear the usual bustling of people outside, the rubber soles of their black synthetic shoes pounding over the grated iron platform. Instead, there is only silence.

Where is everybody?

In a semi-panic, I fling off the bed sheets and plant my feet on the cold floor. The digital clock ticks another minute.

Now I'm eleven minutes late.

A thin film of sweat forms over my forehead and my mind reels with confusion.

Is nobody here?

Breathing quickly now, I lunge for the navy blue sweater and charcoal gray pants crumpled in a pile at the foot of my bed—the standard uniform for all those living in Terra-Mar. I dress hurriedly, wrenching on the shirt that's too tight and slipping into the pants that are too loose. Two black synthetic shoes lay nearby, the laces already double-knotted, and I promptly insert my feet. Acceptably presentable, I turn back around and pull open the heavy metal door.

On the railed platform outside, there's a row of iron pods just like mine. Above them, the crisscrossing fluorescent light bulbs glare down at me, their glowing eyes like eels examining their prey.

An eerie feeling creeps up my spine.

"Ruben?" I call. "Belinda? Chad?"

All I hear in return is silence.

I poke my head out of the door frame and peer toward the pod where my parents sleep. They would usually be leaving to teach the other young minds of the metro right now, but they're nowhere in sight.

In the pitch-black ocean outside, the murky outlines of marine life drift lethargically about, staring inward at the curious bright beacon in the depths of their dark abode. Beyond them, on the sea floor, I can vaguely make out the field of our hydro-powered turbines, their rotors spinning ceaselessly from the relentless ocean currents.

Nothing out of the ordinary there.

I whip around to my other neighboring pod—this one used for the docking of submarines from our cousin settlement, Neptua—looking ahead toward the heart of the metro. There, three giant spheres of hollowed obsidian gleam, suspended above each other by six iron clad bridges in a clockwork formation. They connect to the metro's six locales—Alpha, Beta, Gamma, Delta, Epsilon, and mine, Zeta.

The classrooms, I think, stepping tentatively outside. *They've got to be in one of those.*

I break into a run across the bridge toward the top sphere, my shoes striking heavily against the grated iron floor. The matrix of lights, platforms, and pods flash past me as I call to my friends, "Ruben? Belinda? Chad?" my voice echoing hollowly around me.

Reaching the door at the end of the bridge, I shove it open to find the classroom inside in complete disarray. The desks are flipped onto their sides as if a storm had blown through, and tablet computers litter the area, some of their screens cracked and glowing. On the blackboard, calculus notes are scribbled in white powdery characters.

No bodies, I note, inching through the room. *And no blood, either.*

I kneel down to lift one of the tablets off the floor, sliding the tip of my finger over the darkened screen. A blinking green icon emerges, and I tap it to try and access its memory. Before it can begin loading, though, the screen darkens again. I slide my finger across it once more, but the device no longer responds.

Laying the tablet back on the floor, I maneuver toward door on the opposite side of the room and pull it open. The bridge to Gamma stretches before me, and I race down the path, calling again, "Ruben? Belinda? Chad?"

When I reach the cluster of ashy iron pods there, I rap upon every door in the locale—*bang, bang, bang*—shouting for someone to come out and explain what's going on. When no one does, I round back to the start of the bridge, descending a flight of stairs leading to the mid-level. I cross through the deserted obsidian classroom there—the scene looking exactly like the one above it—toward Zeta. I rap on these doors, but once again find no one present. I repeat the process in almost every locale, calling and pounding and begging for an answer, all to no avail.

Onward I proceed down to Delta, the lowest level. A dent in the network of gridded metal catches my attention and I halt momentarily, but then continue my search for any living soul in the suddenly desolate metro. Peering down over the bridge railings, I search through the abundance of tropical foliage on the ground level, trying to locate the gardeners. Eventually, I descend there, and dash through the groves of fragrant pineapple plants and orchards of leafy lime trees. I pass a dome of jagged quartz crystal and a large steel box in a clearing, but everything around me is vacant.

By the time I return to the door of my own pod, my dirty-blonde hair is matted against my scalp, and I'm panting from exhaustion.

Am I really the only person left in Terra-Mar?

I bend forward to rest my hands on my knees, salty sweat trickling down my forehead and through the gaps between the iron grates below. A hysterical sound bubbles up from my throat, morphing into a winded chuckle.

Nobody's here. Everybody's gone.

The chuckle grows within my throat, eventually transforming into a loud and triumphant laugh.

Nobody's here! Everybody's gone!

"Ha!" I guffaw at the empty space, my body shaking with a mixture of anxiety and giddiness. "Nobody's here! Everybody's gone!"

For eleven years, I've endured the expectations of an entire race of people, and now the pressure is all gone—vanished into thin air. I haven't felt this happy since I first discovered my creating abilities.

Straightening myself, I wipe the perspiration off my temples and push open the door to my pod, muttering excitedly, "I need a submarine to get out of here—a *nuclear* one, like from the past. It doesn't have to be big, just spacious enough for me to walk around. How far is it to the surface from here? I don't know, but I guess I'll find out!"

Less than a minute later, I emerge again lugging a large plastic bag of dried seaweed and vegetables, and an aluminum can of imitation milk—things that I've been saving for the perfect moment to escape from this wretched prison.

Lowering my supplies in front of the entrance to the docking pod, I stare through the glass window at the dimly lit space inside. Nostalgia suddenly washes over me, and I turn back around to my pod. The dusty baseball still rests on the table next to my clock (which now shows 09:50). I hesitate momentarily before grabbing it, then shove it into the ample right pocket of my pants. Leaping back out onto the platform, I retrieve the food supplies and clutch them to my chest—the plastic bag ever-crinkling—before kicking open the door of the docking pod.

A tall rectangular hatch stands opposite the entrance. To the left, a large window displays the endless ocean abyss. On the far end there's a large blue polyurethane sheet draped over a mound of stored tools.

I lower the goods once again and cross the small room to the window, pressing my moist palms against the glass. It's ice cold from the water temperature outside.

"I'll need to rise slowly, though," I warn myself, staring out at the infinite black sea in front of me. Mysterious fanged and finned creatures surely lurk in those eternal shadows. "I have to adjust to the pressure up there, on the surface. I don't want to explode trying to get up there."

I chuckle again, remembering reading from the database in the lab about how anglerfishes' organs expand out of their mouths when they rose too quickly from the bottom of the ocean. My friends and I scrolled through that file about five years ago, when we were bored with trying to understand how time worked. It was the goal that our teacher, Ruben, had set for us.

Of course, I would be fine once I get to the surface. I created this metro to imitate the conditions of the land from the past, or at least my idea of how it must have been. I should have no problem adapting to the pressure up there.

"Alright, now concentrate."

Closing my eyes, I tilt my sweaty forehead against the glass and recall everything I learned about the design and functionality of the most advanced submarines from the past—the hydrodynamic smoothness of the titanium hulls, the sonar and radio controls, the propellers and rudders at the stern, and the engine to bring this amazing vessel to life.

A warming sensation, like the heat from a lamp, spreads down my spine and through my body, all the way to my fingertips and toes. When I feel it, I don't have to open my eyes to know that, outside the metro, there is a powerful invention waiting for me that can withstand the deep sea's freezing temperatures and unforgiving pressure. I know because I formed it from my thoughts alone.

When I finally do open my eyes and peer through the wet splotch that formed on the glass, the dim light radiating out of the pod illuminates the titanic object of my imagination. It's settled within a nest of curled metal beams to prevent the currents from tousling it about. I scan the length of my creation, noting its compact design. Though it isn't large enough to launch a torpedo, it would definitely invoke caution from any of the larger, more aggressive fish in the sea.

When I say that I created everything in Terra-Mar, I mean it literally—I brought them into existence from my mind alone. No tools, no equipment, just like my ancestors did. Creating means to make something out of nothing, and that's exactly what I do. I imagine something, and bring it into existence.

"It's missing something..." I mumble, wrinkling my forehead. Then, I realize. "Ah, I know!"

Closing my eyes and pressing my hands against the glass again, I imagine the sour smell of acrylic paint washing over the submarine's exterior. A few minutes later, I open my eyes to find two words fading into view on the vessel's side.

The Liberation.

That's the name of my submarine, my harbinger to freedom.

A satisfied, if exhausted, grin spreads over my lips as I lower my hands back down, admiring my creation in all its marine glory. I've heard that the sky is blue above the ocean's surface, just like the ocean itself, and have even viewed images of its beauty from the metro's infinite database. Now, I'll be able to see it with my own eyes.

I can't wait, I think eagerly, practically salivating at the idea.

A sudden *clang* startles me, and I spin around toward the open door. But in accordance with the rest of the morning, there's no one on the platform, nothing to explain the noise. Before I can turn back to the submarine, the *clang* comes again, now closer and more disconcerting.

With horror, I turn my attention up to the metal grid above Alpha, where a dent curves inward like a swelling bubble. Within it, a small area of glass begins to crack.

"What the—"

The glass shatters, flooding my home with gallons of sea water by the thousands.

"Whoa!" I cry in panic and slap myself frantically against the window.

I created the enclosure to be indestructible. No amount of pressure from the ocean floor is supposed to break through to the metro. How is this happening?

For a moment I can only stare wide-eyed at the ocean rushing in. But then I snap back into myself.

I need to get out of here *right now.*

Clenching my eyes shut, I concentrate as hard as I can on the sound of grinding gears, ignoring a third *clang* that echoes dangerously from somewhere else in the metro. Opening my eyes again, I'm relieved to see the submarine's metallic bridge extending out from above its name—the opening only about ten feet away.

My escape is so close.

Hopping anxiously up to the hatch, I grab the wheel at its center and yank to unlock it, but just as I do, a clattering of metal sounds from across the room. Jumping again in alarm, I scan the wall, expecting to see it imploding. I brace myself for the torrent of water, but instead, a silver wrench skids across the floor from the pile of tools, stopping a few inches from my shoe. Looking out from beneath the cloth are five pairs of eyes.

"AH!" I scream, wheeling my arms backward and stumbling into the plastic bag of dried vegetables. With a *crunch* I crush them to dust and hit the wall hard, my body throttling from the impact. I watch in astonishment as five young boys wriggle out from beneath the sheet, dispersing the tools noisily everywhere—*clank, clank, clank.*

"Wh-where'd you guys come from?" I yelp in surprise, clinging onto the sleek iron behind me like a lifeline. "I thought everyone was gone. Have you been hiding here this whole time?"

One of the boys, his fluffy blonde hair waving atop a doughy face, bounces up to me and fixes his bright hazel eyes on mine. The crown of his head barely reaches my belly. He puffs his little chest out authoritatively, the fabric of his sweater scarcely expanding, and balls his small fists by his pants.

"You have to get us out of here!" he demands in a low voice that is undoubtedly forced to make him sound older. "You're supposed to save us from destruction, because you're the Creator!"

I make a face. I hate it when people call me that.

"Who – what – how—" I sputter in outrage, flailing my arms in an attempt to regain my composure.

This is all too much to absorb at once—the Terra-Marans' disappearance, the breach in the enclosure, and now a little boy telling me what to do. I hadn't counted on any of this happening when I went to sleep last night. I thought that I'd wake up to another tedious day of tests and experiments—but not *this.*

Finally recovering from the shock, I straighten my posture and look down at the boy. "Who are you guys? Where'd you all come from? What happened to everyone else?"

The tools clack and jingle as another boy worms out from his peers to stand next to the blonde boy.

"There's no time for questions, Creator!" He plants his hands dictatorially on his small hips. "Terra-Mar's deteriorating, and you have a duty to protect the future generations of Builders!"

I glance through the docking pod's entrance to the top of the enclosure, where the ocean continues to flood inside. With each passing second, the edges of the broken glass widens further, yielding to the force of the ocean. Below, I can see the tops of the trees submerging beneath the water.

Dammit, I grit my teeth and look between the damaged glass and my submarine outside the window. I really wanted to go up to the surface alone, but I can't leave these boys behind.

Slapping one hand over my forehead, I give in. "Alright, you're all coming with me."

"Yes!" a third boy cheers as he scrambles up to his companions. Two more boys follow him from beneath the cloth, rejoicing in their escape.

All five of them now line up in front of me as if anticipating a class.

Before I can turn back to the hatch, there's another *clang*—this one so close that it vibrates my bones. Looking back out of the open door, I see a veil of water raging down from above, splashing wildly through the grated iron platform. Outside, the submarine's bridge reaches the hatch's frame and locks against it with a loud, *clunk.* A whirring sound follows as it drains the water within.

The metro is crumbling fast. I need to open the hatch *now.*

Impatiently, I sprint for the wheel of the hatch, grabbing the curved sides and straining as hard as I can.

"What're you doing?" one of the boys asks in panic.

"Guys," I grunt, my arms shaking from the tension of my muscles, "I'm going to open the hatch now. Step back and wait until the water empties from the bridge, then run as fast as you can get into the submarine."

"*What?!*" the wavy-haired boy cries in disbelief, running up to my side as the wheel jerks roughly in my grasp. "But the water in the bridge—"

The wheel slackens under my weight, and I tumble onto the floor, landing agonizingly on my left side. Before I can prepare myself, the hatch flies open, knocking painfully into my belly. A wave of icy-cold ocean water swallows me, the momentum sending my body rolling helplessly backward. After a moment the water settles and I gasp for air, thrashing my sodden hair back from my face. The boys stare back at me with dread, their pants soaked to the knee. Around us, the tools from the pile—hammers, wrenches, saws, and screwdrivers—disperse from the sudden onrush, gleaming in the dim light like limp fish.

"Go! Get in, already!" I urge the boys, waving one soaking arm frantically toward the open bridge.

Hastily, the boys shuffle inside, leaping over the tools and shrieking at each other to hurry up. One of them accidentally steps onto a wrench and trips, hitting the floor with a *thunk*, but quickly clambers back up to his feet to follow after his peers. Before he disappears inside, I manage to swipe my food supply—now floating next to me—and holler at him, "Wait! Take this!"

The child stops in his tracks and spins around in my direction, his mouth gaping wide in distress. He races back to grab the bag and hauls it away into the dark, the plastic bag crinkling loudly in his nervous fingers. At the end of the bridge, the other four boys cluster around the closed hatch of the submarine, banging incessantly on it.

"How do you open this thing?" one of them complains.

"Did you even know what you were doing when you created this?" another gripes.

"Open it just like I opened the hatch here in the docking pod!" I snap, annoyed at their ignorance. I flap my sodden sleeves vigorously, even though they aren't looking at me. "Turn the wheel to the left, then push it open. Once you're inside, spin it the opposite direction to lock it. Lefty-loosy, righty-tighty, remember?"

Before I catch the boys' response, another freezing wave knocks me over from behind, jarring me against the wall.

Why the hell am I still here? I think, frustrated. Now knee-deep in water, I climb dizzily to my feet and thrust myself toward the open hatch. When I finally manage to get into the bridge, I grab the wheel on the other side of the hatch and fight against the rushing force of the water to drag it shut.

The bridge is now completely shrouded in darkness.

The boys' baffled voices echo from the submarine entrance at the other end—they still haven't opened the other hatch.

I run for the opposite end, my feet splashing noisily through the water that flowed in from the docking pod. Near the middle of the bridge, I trip over something, and find myself soaring forward onto my outstretched arms. I'm met with a mouthful of salty water.

"Ow, you stepped on my foot!" one of the boys shouts at me.

"Well, I can't exactly see in the dark!" I bark back, spitting out the salt water. Pushing myself to my feet, I brush back my wet hair and continue on to the end of the bridge, slower this time in case of other obstructions. I squeeze through the cluster of little protesting bodies there to grasp the wheel of the submarine hatch. Heaving my torso leftward, I feel the wheel ease loose until it spins freely. The hatch now open, I shove hastily inside, bringing the numbingly cold water in with me. Bright fluorescent lights flicker on above, revealing a small entry area with another hatch at the right and, opposite that, a ladder leading up through a small hole in the ceiling.

Behind me, the boys shriek with nervousness as they enter the vessel. I wait impatiently for the one at the back to trail in with our food supply, then slam the hatch shut and whirl back around toward the ladder.

Emerging into the main control room, I dive for a glowing blue button secured behind a transparent case. It's set among other glowing buttons beneath a disorienting array of pressure gauges—all of them indicating that the sub is stable. Squeezing the sides of the case, I flip it open and slap the blue button violently. Outside, the bridge whirrs as it detaches from the metro and withdraws back to the submarine.

Slamming the case shut again, I bound for a sleek metallic panel at my right, past the expansive window displaying the opaque sea. Above the panel hangs a medium-sized computer screen with bright green numbers trickling down it like raindrops. And just over that is a large yellow clock that tells me it's almost 10:30.

Focusing on the panel, I flip on a pair of high beams, and two streaks of light come surging from beneath the window. They illuminate a group of ghostly long-tailed fish swimming hurriedly away. With a gentle press of my hand, I ease another lever forward, initiating a burst of electricity through the machine's nuclear veins as the engine hums to life. The propellers begin rotating in the stern, and a sliding sensation overtakes me.

The Liberation is starting to move, floating out from the nest outside the docking pod.

Switching to a new lever, I drive the watercraft leftward, rounding the submarine back around Terra-Mar, which remains in view through the panoramic window. Behind me, the boys push into the room, their wet shoes squeaking on the ladder. They talk over each other loudly, exclaiming about the chaos around the ship.

"Look!"

"It's Terra-Mar."

"It's being destroyed!"

They cluster up against the glass, creating a puddle of seawater at their feet. I have to look over their heads to see the damage, but it with the glow of the submarine's side beams, isn't hard to spot. A crippling wave of despair hits me as I watch the metro implode—the glass enclosure shattering into a million glittering pieces, the network of gridded metal twisting into an unrecognizable gnarled sculpture, the three obsidian classrooms lying ruined in the sand. The entirety of Terra-Mar is reduced to an iron skeleton, its matrix of fluorescent lights fizzling into darkness.

In the blink of an eye, everything I've ever known is gone.

I don't understand, I think in disbelief. *I created Terra-Mar to withstand centuries of pressure and nearly sub-zero temperatures According to everything I've learned about physics, the metro was bound to exist forever.*

But apparently I was wrong.

I now have nothing by which to remember the lost Terra-Marans, not even the time machine.

....

The ocean is so dark that the high beams barely make a difference.

Reaching up to the computer screen, I press a glowing yellow button and send a few sonar clicks ahead of me. Seeing no disruption among the trickling green numbers, I grasp the driving lever and inch it further forward. The sub bucks under me regardless, and I slide backward slightly as the vessel accelerates boldly ahead. With a tilt of my wrist, I guide The Liberation upward, toward the grand and glorious surface.

There's nothing holding me back now.

"We've got to find the Terra-Marans!" one of the boys declares, breaking my concentration. "They're out there somewhere! They could still be alive!"

Exasperatedly, I peer over my shoulder at a child with straight blonde hair and pointy chin. "No they couldn't. If they didn't escape, they've drowned by now."

"Somebody came into the metro this morning and *took* them!"

another boy answers, his shoes squeaking on the sodden floor as he bounces up to the other.

"*Took* them?" I ridicule, arching a disbelieving brow. "What do you mean *took* them?"

"A bunch of mean-looking people made holes in the enclosure. They came in and told everyone to go with them, or else they'd rip them to shreds!"

"We were on our way to class," the boy who carried the food supply explains shyly. "We hid in the docking pod because we knew they wouldn't be leaving through there."

"That makes no sense," I retort, turning back to the limitless ocean in front of me. "I designed Terra-Mar so that the docking pod would be the *only* point of entry. Nobody can enter through any other means."

"Well, *they* did!" the pointy-chinned boy says haughtily. "They set up invisible bridges outside the enclosure and made *holes* in it, then came inside to force the Terra-Marans into their invisible submarines, and sealed the holes again when they left."

"Who're *'they',* anyway?" I've only been with these kids for a few minutes, and they're already getting on my nerves. Nothing they say sounds remotely possible by any scientific means.

"We don't know. We just ran, and hid."

"They're probably *Scatters,*" another boy sneers. "No other kind of people would be crazy enough to *abduct* us."

I fall silent at the word. For as long as I've lived, I've never enjoyed belittling Scatters—the rejects of Terra-Mar. They're just clumsy people who made lots of mistakes when building things. All of them were humble and meek—traits which the Terra-Marans for some reason considered to be useless and even destructive.

But the Scatters never looked mean to me, I think, lowering my troubled gaze to the levers. *They looked just, well, miserable, because they're incapable of finishing anything they start. That, and they're always accidentally ruining what a Builder begins. I could understand them being frustrated, but not mean.*

But how else would everyone have disappeared if they weren't abducted? I can't help but wonder if the Scatters are somehow behind the Terra-Marans' mysterious absence.

Sudden holes in the enclosure certainly would have compromised

Terra-Mar's infrastructure. But only one person would have known how to make those holes in the first place.

My forehead wrinkles, and my breathing halts.

No, I think uneasily. *It couldn't be him... could it?*

"Where are we going, anyway?" one of the boys cuts into my thoughts.

I shoot an accusing glare at him before turning back to the screen of trickling green numbers. "Terra-Mar is gone. I'm taking us up to the surface."

The children fall quiet.

"But..." one of them begins anxiously. "They're our fellow Terra-Marans! You have to find them! You're the Creator, after all!"

Making a face, I turn around to find the children lined up once again in a neat row.

"I do have a name, you know," I snap irritably at them, "and it's Alan. Not Creator. *Alan!*"

"Creator, you have a duty to preserve the legacy of the Builders!" the blonde dough-faced boy says earnestly, as if I'd never spoken.

"Oh, *nooooo way,*" I chuckle wryly and turn back to the control panel to increase the submarine's speed. "I've waited far too long to get out of that place—to *be rid* of my creative duties. Now that Terra-Mar is destroyed, I can do whatever I want."

The boys gasp.

"But you can't just *abandon* them!"

"They depend on you for *everything!*"

"Exactly," I agree. "I'm done having people depend on me. If the Terra-Marans want to be saved, they'll have to build their own way out for once."

"But without the Terra-Marans," the pointy-chinned boy says. "You would've never discovered your ability to create!"

My lips flatten to a straight line as a pang of guilt streaks through me.

He's right, of course. Without Ruben's help, I would never have discovered what I could do. He was the one who helped me make my first creation. It was an ability he took advantage of, but an ability no less. I owe him.

"Fine," I huff. "We'll look for them."

The boys burst into cheers, and I cringe even more.

Great, I think. *Now, I'm stuck with these kids for who knows how long it takes to track down the people of the metro.*

Pulling both driving levers, I tip The Liberation back to a flat altitude and slow the propellers to an easy cruise so I can make the loop around the old site of Terra-Mar. When we're safely churning in the direction we came, I cross my arms over my chest and sit back on the panel's edge, regarding each boy sternly.

"Alright, since I'm going to be stuck with you little jerks for a while, it would be helpful if you told me your names."

"I'm Shawn," the first boy says proudly, grinning a set of pearly-white teeth.

"And I'm Lawrence," the dough-faced boy says.

"My name is Cal," a dark-skinned boy says on the other side of Shawn, straightening himself to a confident posture.

"And I'm Beckett!" the pointy-chinned kid introduces. He jumps up and down excitedly, making the vessel rock slightly. I frown at him until he stops.

The last boy is the one who carried the food—the shy one. He opens his mouth to introduce himself, but before he can speak, Lawrence steps forward and points over at him. "That's Owen. He's usually quiet and just listens to people most of the time. He's seven—one year older than the rest of us."

His words robbed from him, Owen looks disappointedly at the moist floor.

I put my hands on my hips. "Well, guys, if we're going to do this together there a few things we need to get straight. You're in *my* submarine, and that means you have to listen to *my* rules. I need you all to behave when you're in here so that everything can operate smoothly. Every little thing you do will have a big impact on me, each other, and the vessel itself. You need to be *really careful* when—"

But before I can finish my speech on watercraft safety, the boys disperse zealously to the far regions of the room and begin tinkering with the knobs and levers I designed so meticulously in my head.

"Ooh, what does this do?" Cal wonders aloud, attempting to pry open the case to a glowing red button.

"No, don't touch that!" I shout in panic, reaching out to grab him.

"Is this a sonar machine?" Beckett asks eagerly as he bounces—*thud, thud, thud*—toward the control panel at the bottom of the screen. "Can I click it next time?"

"No, you can't!" I cry over at him, veering sharply away from Cal to shoo Beckett from the screen. "And stop jumping like that! It's disruptive to—"

"What kind of a screen doesn't show images?" Lawrence derides, darting excitedly up to the panel behind Beckett.

"The layout of this room isn't efficient," Owen proposes innocently. "I can help you build a better one if you want me to."

"Can this thing go any faster?" Shawn joins in behind Lawrence and Beckett at the control panel—their necks barely reaching the top edge. He extends one hand dangerously over his companions' shoulders, preparing to grasp the levers.

My eyes bulge and I lunge forward, plucking all three boys by their sweater collars and dragging them—kicking and screaming—to the far end of the room. As we pass Cal—who's still attempting to pry open the safety case—I scoop him up too and drag him along.

These kids have the attention spans of guppies.

"Hey, I was looking at that!" Shawn exclaims, straining against my grip and writhing defiantly in my hands. His sweater stretches to the point of tearing.

"Why can't I click the sonar?" Beckett howls.

"Your screen is *broken!*" Lawrence wails, rocking his body violently back and forth.

"You weren't looking at them—you were going to *touch* them. And no, you can't click the sonar. And no, my screen is *not broken!*"

I wrestle all four of them toward the hole in the floor. Seeing me approach, Owen scurries sheepishly away from the window to the side of the hole.

I pant from the struggle, but make sure to look them straight in the eye as I point down through the hole. "Get back down there now! I can't have you messing up everything I created or I'll have to spend all my time fixing these tools instead of actually *using* them!"

Shawn, Beckett, Lawrence, and Cal whine infuriatingly, but Owen simply frowns.

"This is so dumb!" Shawn cries, balling his fists by his sides. Beside him, Cal sighs and flings his arms exasperatedly above his head.

"Yeah," Beckett agrees. "We can't do *anything* in here!"

Lawrence begins to stomp—*clunk, clunk, clunk*—on the wet floor, splashing water everywhere.

"If you don't like the way I run this vessel, then be my guest—" I point through the window to the unending, opaque sea. "See if you can fend for yourselves."

The boys fall abruptly silent, clearly trying to gauge whether I'm serious. Rather than risk it, they slump through the hole one by one, grumbling among themselves the entire way. Owen is predictably the last to go.

When they reach the bottom, they hop off of the ladder with five nerve-wracking *pangs*, sending water spraying up from the puddle around them and making me even more infuriated.

"Be *quiet*!" I holler irately, poking my head through the hole. My face burns as they giggle tauntingly back up at me.

"Don't forget that whoever abducted the Terra-Marans had submarines, so they'll be able to detect the sound levels of other submarines—like *this one*," I spit vehemently. "If you guys are being loud and rowdy, they'll know that we're coming. Maybe they'll kidnap us too, or just take the Terra-Marans so far away that you'll never see them again! You want that to happen? Huh?"

Finally understanding my point, the boys cast their eyes shamefully down at the floor, falling silent again.

Sighing wearily, I climb down to the sorry children. When I reach the bottom—stepping my already-wet feet cautiously onto the puddled floor so I don't slip—the five of them part to let me through. I walk to the hatch at the opposite wall, against which slumps the neglected bag of dried food and its companion, the aluminum can. Gripping the wheel at the hatch's center, I heave it leftward and—with a grunt—push it open.

"Behold," I proclaim, my arms spread out in mock enthusiasm. "Your bedroom."

In front of me is a narrow room with a single pull-out bed which, when laid flat, encompasses half of the room's width. At the far end is a sink with a faucet that dispenses desalinated water from the ocean outside. Behind this is another hatch, closed to conceal The Liberation's humming engine room.

With a hesitant shuffle, the boys peek in around me.

"You call this a bedroom?" Shawn ridicules disdainfully.

"You call this a *bed?*" Beckett derides.

I cross my arms, feeling slightly offended. For having only narrowly escaped kidnapping and death, these boys sure are high maintenance.

"The Liberation's sole purpose is to travel quickly and quietly through the water, and the living quarter is built to be *efficient,* not *comfortable.*"

"But there's only *one* bed!" Cal complains, still in the entry area behind me. "How're all of us going to fit on that thing?"

"Well, I didn't count on anyone joining me," I glower over my shoulder at him. "But since you guys are here now, I guess I have to make some adjustments."

Turning back to the bedroom, I close my eyes and open my palms toward the walls, concentrating on the feeling of hard, unyielding titanium softened by a plush mattress. The warming sensation surges down my spine, through my arms and legs, and into my fingertips and toes.

Soon, the groan of metal fills my ears as two slabs protrude from the walls. Then comes the soft *thunk* of three thin mattresses flopping onto the bed frames like loaves of bread.

The boys gasp in awe (as people usually do when watching me use my ability), and I lower my hands to my hips, my task complete. The boys leap ecstatically toward my latest creations, and clamber over each other to reach the top two beds, bouncing on them once they get up there. Their wet shoes soak into the fabric of the mattresses as they shriek with glee, to my continued dismay.

"Yay, we've all got beds now!" Beckett cheers, jumping up and down on the left bunk bed, his head nearly hitting the ceiling. The force of his bouncing knocks Owen off balance behind him, and he falls forward onto his hands and knees, almost toppling over the edge. The sheepish boy catches himself just before this happens, and peers angrily over at his friend, who continues jumping ignorantly.

"Wait, no we don't!" Cal complains, stopping in his tracks. He looks accusingly at me. "There are only *four* bunk beds, but there are *five* of us. We need another bed so that *all* of us can sleep here!"

"Well," I sigh, resting my hands on my waist. "The rest of the vessel is for operations, so if you don't like floating around in a bunch of seawater in the ballast, I suggest that two of you *share* one of the beds."

"Nooo!" Lawrence gripes.

"That's so unfair!" Shawn stops now to sit at the edge of the bed, holding his head disappointedly in his hands.

"I don't want sleep with someone else!" Beckett whines. He shoots a conspicuous look at Owen across the room.

"Well, *deal* with it," I huff and turn around to the exit. "Be grateful that I made beds for you at all!"

"But where're *you* going to sleep, Alan?" Owen asks timidly.

With one foot out in the entryway, I turn back to the boys, "In the control room, of course. Now go to sleep."

Before the boys can argue, I spring out of the entryway and slam the hatch shut behind me. Spinning the wheel closed, I hear five futile *pangs* as the boys beat their fists against the wall, demanding that I let them out. After the hatch is locked, I fetch the plastic bag and can off the floor and tuck them under one arm before ascending the ladder once again.

Emerging back into the control room, I toss the food supply haphazardly into a corner and resume my position at the control panel.

The vast waters stretch in front of me—the occasional fish flitting quickly by—as I replay the devastation of my most sophisticated creation in my mind, recalling everything from the first dent in the gridded metal to the metro's final collapse.

Suddenly, the soreness of my muscles invades my consciousness, and I realize what an exhausting ordeal I've endured just to get onto The Liberation, not to mention bringing those five very difficult children with me. I wonder what kind of mattress I want to create for myself here, in the control room—one with springs or one that's made of memory-foam?

My heart sinks as I realize that I feel absolutely no despair for what happened to Terra-Mar. After all, I've hated it for the last eleven years, and now that I'm no longer responsible for it, my shoulders feel lighter, and my spirits, higher. I promised those kids that I'd help find the Terra-Marans, but it's the last thing in the world I want to do.

"Why do I have to be so nice?" I sigh, shaking my head, and take hold of the right lever. Inching it forward, the submarine speeds ahead, the sediments of the ocean passing as ghostly blurs at the side windows.

Even if the Terra-Marans are dead, I think morbidly. *At least I'll know for certain.*

The sooner I find out what happened to them, the sooner I can see that blue sky.

PART 1

CHAPTER 1

I made my first creation when I was six years old. It was back in the early days of Terra-Mar, during Ruben's lecture on literature of the past. There used to be only one classroom—an oddly-shaped clump of spiky quartz lumped arbitrarily together from the remains of our ancestors' space crafts. It stood at the center of the ground level (the *only* level in our settlement at that time) and served as a place for us to satiate our minds when there wasn't enough food to satiate our stomachs. The classroom's one light source was a large fluorescent lamp that hung down through a hole in the ceiling. Its thin wire snaked out onto the salty ground, connecting beneath the soil to the small field of hydro-powered turbines nearby. After centuries of green algae accumulation on the glass, we could barely see the turbines, but as long as the lights were shining we knew that they were still operating.

There were no desks back then. Instead, we had wispy slabs of steel bent into makeshift tables a foot above the dirt. For lack of chairs, we sat or knelt on the rough ground, often suffering from numb legs and feet. Our feet were completely bare because our ancestors' leather sandals had worn away long ago. The clothes that we did have were terribly faded—you could hardly make out the colors of the blue and orange robes.

Ruben was the only teacher at that time, since everyone else's efforts were reserved for nursing the young and old, and farming the few fruiting plants we had that bloomed in the heavily salinized soil.

With the bottom of his lengthy robe dragging in the dust, Ruben paced back and forth before me and my classmates, squinting at an old tablet computer through a pair of eyeglasses. They belonged to one of his greatest grandfathers and couldn't have been anything close to the prescription he needed, but he wore them regardless. Ruben had required us to read a story called "Shoeless Joe" by a writer named W. P. Kinsella who was obsessed with an arcane game called "baseball." Ruben was reciting some brief phrases from the text that were downloaded from our ancestors' database long-ago.

When the growling of my belly didn't occupy my attention, the teacher's drawling voice caused my mind to wander. I leaned my elbows forward onto my desk and propped my head lazily in my hands, only half-listening to Ruben drone on about all the places I'd never visit, the people I'd never know, and the things that the author had done in his lifetime that I would never do because I didn't live on the surface. No one did anymore, not since the mountain peaks were swallowed by the sea hundreds of years ago.

I began asking myself what it would be like to go to a place like "Iowa," to meet people like "Babe Ruth" and to watch a "Red Sox game" in a "stadium." According to what I'd read about the ball itself (and from looking at the images Ruben downloaded for us), it was crafted from a rubber center, wrapped with several layers of yarn, thrown into some sort of spinning drum that painted it white, and then finally stitched together with two flaps of white leather.

What would it be like to hold that ball? I'd thought dreamily, the heads of my classmates blurring into a dreamy haze. *To feel the leather in my hands, to smell the varnish wafting up into my nostrils—to actually "pitch" it to someone?*

And then the warming sensation happened—surging down my spine, through my shoulders and back, along my arms and legs toward my fingertips and toes.

When my eyes refocused, there was something on the desk in front of me. To my astonishment, I saw a pristine baseball sitting between my hands, complete with bright red stitches.

My breath caught and I snapped back to attention. Where did this thing come from? Had someone put it there when I dozed off? How did they manage to get one that looked so new?

From the corner of his eye, Ruben noticed my unease and stopped pacing, fixing his copper-brown eyes in my direction.

"You've got something to show us, Alan?" I could tell he wasn't pleased by my distraction.

Several students turned their sunken cheeks to stare at me, some of their stomachs growling loudly with hunger.

Motioning weakly to the baseball on my tablet, I cleared my throat to say something, but couldn't come up with the right words.

Ruben' forehead wrinkled as he studied the object in front of me, his dark brows pinning together over his lenses. Like me, he clearly knew what the object *was,* just not how it *got here.*

"It's a baseball," observed Belinda, a girl sitting nearby. She had long, flaming red hair that hung down to the middle of her back. She was a favorite among the boys. "Like from the book—a sphere stitched together with two strips of white leather. Alan has a baseball."

I felt myself blush with more than just embarrassment.

The boy directly in front of me turned, his interest piqued.

"Wow," Sal said. "How'd you make it, Alan? We don't have any rubber, or paint, or even thread. How did you do it?"

The other twelve eyes in the classroom turned to me.

"I don't know," I muttered. "I just imagined it." I tried to turn my attention back to my glowing tablet screen in an attempt to look like I was studying, but to no avail. My classmates leaned into each other, murmuring excitedly.

"He just *imagined* it?" they asked one another.

"Does that mean he *thought* it into being?"

I glanced up at Ruben, expecting to see a look of disapproval. Instead, I found a small smile peeking out from under his beard, his eyes alight with pride.

Without breaking his gaze, he announced bluntly, "Class is dismissed. Everyone except for Alan, please leave the room."

The students rose, shooting confused glances at me as they patted dust off their robes and filed quietly out. After a moment, it was just me and my teacher.

Feeling uneasy, I rose from my desk as well, not daring to touch the baseball.

"Walk with me, Alan," Ruben said, motioning me toward one of the exits. "We have a lot to talk about."

....

Outside the classroom, the fluorescent light bulbs above glowed dim and warm in an "X" formation, illuminating the meager gardens at the outskirts of the perimeter, where the Terra-Marans worked scrupulously to cultivate the scarce vegetation. I could see my parents on the far end of the clearing. They struggled with a desalinater, squeezing the swollen rubber bag attached to a tiny outlet in the enclosure to spread sweet, potable water onto their garden of sprouting kale leaves. Even from this distance, I could see my mother's freckles against her fair skin—it was a trait she passed on to me. My father gave me his mop of dark gold hair.

A few feet away from them, a black box crackled with static as it searched the surrounding area for radio waves from Neptua's submarines—it was the last remaining server from our ancestors' space crafts.

Life in Terra-Mar was much more difficult when I was young. In addition to the shortage of food, there was no network of metal supporting the enclosure, as our ancestors had used the last of their inventory. Instead, the glass was an irregularly-formed dome that broke frequently from pressure overload, which we had to patch quickly and ungracefully with chunky pieces of glass that were prepared in advance for such occurrences. Through our radio correspondences with Neptua, we heard their settlement looked even worse.

For ten awkward minutes, Ruben and I silently circled the area outside the classroom, surveying the grim sights. A dull pain throbbed in my temple, warning me of an oncoming headache (they were common down here due to the gravitational density) and I rubbed my fingertips lightly over it.

"Our numbers are dwindling, Alan," Ruben told me, hugging his trusty tablet to his chest. I strained to hear him over the cries of the babies, who were barely able to nurse from their mothers' deflated breasts. "We weren't meant to live down here, halfway to hell, where the warmth of the sunlight never reaches us. We evolved to thrive up there, among mountains and valleys, beneath clear blue skies. But all that's gone now, after hundreds of years of destruction. We need to expand our numbers and create space for us to grow here in the ocean depths. We need to take back our earth."

I dropped the hand at my temple, feeling like I'd exacerbated my headache rather than soothed it.

"We've always been different from the rest of creation," my teacher continued, his normally monotonous drawl rising in excitement. "We can build things: houses, vehicles, cities—even colonies in the remotest parts of the solar system."

Ruben fell silent as we passed the famished mothers still trying to suckle their children. An infant screeched, sending a sharp pain streaking through my nerves and bringing my headache to new light. Rubbing my temple again, I fell one step behind my teacher as we proceeded on toward the radio again, beside which stood a titanium alloy hatch built into the glass. Glancing briefly at it, I recalled the rumors—apparently it had only ever being opened when our cousins from Neptua came to take Scatters to the Scatter settlement (the place where those who could not build were exiled). It hadn't happened since decades before my birth, though, so the Neptuans were nothing but a fantasy to me, along with the Scatters.

When my teacher suddenly stopped in his tracks, I did too, frowning intensely from the pain in my head. I took a few deep breaths and looked up at him. He wore a grave expression, his eyes darkening as he gazed at the film of fuzzy green algae on the uneven glass above my parents.

"How did it happen?" Ruben asked, his voice deep and foreboding. "How did you bring that baseball into being?"

I hesitated, choosing my words carefully,

"I-I was just listening to you talk about 'Shoeless Joe'," I stammered. "I remembered the research that we did for it—the history of baseball, how the baseball was made—and then it just..." I paused, feeling embarrassed. "And then it just *existed*."

Ruben was quiet, nodding ponderously.

"So you create by understanding the creation," he concluded. "How it works, what it's made of, the purpose of its existence, etcetera..."

I held my breath. Had I done something bad? Was I not supposed to create things?

"What you did in class today," Ruben began ominously, clenching his tablet tighter in his arm. "You know what that means, don't you?"

I gulped. Would I be sent to the Scatter settlement for this?

Behind us, another baby screeched and I gritted my teeth. My head was pounding.

Finally, Ruben looked down at me, his copper eyes blazing with what looked like ambition. He knelt down on one knee to match my height and placed his tablet on the ground, something he *never* did for fear that he or someone else may accidentally step on it. With both hands, he held my shoulders and looked directly into my eyes.

"What you did back in the classroom, Alan, was something special.

Your ability is a gift—a blessing. With it, you can help us survive the blight of this place. You can *save* us, Alan."

I sucked in an anxious breath. Me? Save us? I could hardly pay attention in class, let alone rescue the human race from extinction. Why was Ruben telling me all this?

"I, but, I..." I tried and failed to formulate a half-sensible response to this completely insensible situation.`

Suddenly an unsettling *crack* came from my right, and I whipped around to see the glass directly above my parents shatter, engulfing them in gallons of icy ocean water.

"No!" I screamed, and dashed toward my mother and father just as the tide slammed into me, knocking me off my feet. For a few seconds I tumbled backward in the current, flailing wildly. Finally grabbing onto what felt like solid earth, I dragged myself to my feet, shivering and blinking away sea water. When I opened my eyes, chaos surrounded me.

My parents had clambered, unharmed, from beneath the spilling break, but their garden was completely submerged in the relentless onrush of water. After eight months of cultivation, everything they'd worked for was washed away in the wreckage. Behind them, my classmates scrambled for the sturdier parts of the enclosure while the mothers cried in fright, clutching their now-wailing babies to their bosoms as the water gathered around them.

On the opposite side of the enclosure, a group of Terra-Marans who'd been tending to their crops splashed toward a collection of haphazardly blown glass slabs and torches. They carried them toward the break, enduring the punishing surge of freezing liquid as they held the slabs up to block the opening. After a moment, the torch-bearers were able to activate the flame and begin the sealing process.

The settlement was an utter mess. We'd seen cracks like this in the past, but every time it happened they got progressively worse. Even now, the torch-bearers were barely able to lessen the crushing stream of sea water coming in. The enclosure was our only source of protection against the toxic planet we called home, and we were about to lose it.

"Your ability, Alan," Ruben's voice soared over the pandemonium.

I turned to see him standing near the classroom calmly despite the quickly rising water, which had soaked him to his knees. His tablet glowed beneath the rippling waves, its screen flickering until it turned black altogether.

"But it's just my imagination!" I shouted back. "It's not real!"

Another *crack* sounded and I swung around to see a second bout of ocean water cascading through the enclosure, pummeling the helpless mothers and their babes in its icy grasp.

Some of the Terra-Marans at the first break plunged their hands into the water to gather the remaining glass slabs and started heaving through the ebb toward the second crack, but halfway there, they stopped. I saw the hope drain from their faces as they watched the thrashing bodies of the infants float away with the current. They knew what we all knew—patching the enclosure at this point was impossible.

What little warmth was left in my body evaporated as one simple thought materialized in my consciousness:

This was it. Right here, after millennia of evolving, civilizing, building, and innovating, we were all going to die.

"Imagine a better world, Alan," my teacher shouted. Despite the hysteria that surrounded us, his eyes were focused exclusively on me.

"Sand and heat," he said, holding my gaze. "Sand and heat."

"Sand and heat?" I muttered back at him, confused. "What are you talking about?"

For a moment, I stood frozen, the water around me rising perilously higher. Ruben's laser-focused stare willed me to understand, his eyebrows cinched together in concentration.

Then, all at once, I understood.

Reaching my hands out toward the first break, I closed my eyes, imagining the graininess of sand in my palms and the piercing heat of a torch as it melted the sand into a sleek consistency. The warming sensation I'd felt in the classroom returned, and a few seconds later, the deafening rush of incoming water softened.

When I looked up, a transparent patch of glass had covered the first void in the algae-riddled enclosure, cutting off the torrential downpour of seawater. The fallen Terra-Marans beneath it gaped and murmured, turning their dripping faces back and forth as they searched for the source of the glass. Eventually they noticed me from across the enclosure, my arms still outstretched, and their eyes grew wide with awe.

Had I just done what they thought I did? Bring something into being using only my mind?

But I didn't have time to answer questions—there was still another crack in the enclosure.

Whirling around to the second break, I looked past the mothers wading frantically toward their shrieking babies and aimed my hands up at the shattered glass. I shut my eyes, concentrated on the mended surface, and within seconds, the sound of rushing water faded completely, leaving nothing but the astonished voices of the Terra-Marans to fill the air.

Opening my eyes once more, I saw a crowd of eyes staring back at me.

In that instant I realized the implications of what I'd just done. I'd saved my people from certain death, and they knew it. They were indebted to me, and my life would never be the same because of it. In a matter of seconds, I had transformed from a starving young boy at the bottom of the sea to a pillar of hope for a dying community.

"Behold," Ruben said, the ambitious flame returning to his eyes. "My student—the Creator."

And from that day forward, that was my name.

Creator.

....

In the months that followed, the Terra-Marans resumed their work around the enclosure with renewed hope for the future. Miraculously, Ruben was able to nurse his waterlogged tablet back to life, and he used it to teach me everything he could about the architecture of the past. The Golden Gate Bridge, the Akashi-Kaikyo Bridge, the Millau Viaduct—he downloaded images of each and showed me what made their designs effective and iconic.

After studying the skill of compounding metal into alloys, I chose to use iron to create the three levels of Terra-Mar, and extended the enclosure so that the platforms and bridges shot upward toward its summit, like plants stretching up toward the sun (though I'd only ever seen such a phenomenon from computer recordings). I reinforced the glass's thickness, and strengthened it with a skeleton of gridded metal, ensuring that no breaks would ever occur again.

I made it absolutely indestructible.

Across the three levels, I created the six locales of Terra-Mar, and outfitted them with individual pods. I created electric stoves, sinks that dispensed potable water, spinning laundry machines, showers, toilets, and a septic system that delivered waste down beneath the ground to fertilize our gardens.

At Ruben's suggestion, I created three large spheres of obsidian—the stone of truth— and positioned them all at the center of each level. I hollowed their cores to fill them with desks and chalkboards, and created more tablet computers to replace the ones that were destroyed on the day of my first creation.

Most importantly, I expanded the field of hydro-powered turbines outside the enclosure to accommodate the growing size of the settlement. The ocean—once the greatest threat to our livelihood—now became our main source of energy.

I saw everything that I had made, and it was very good.

Terra-Mar quickly began to prosper, along with its people's spirits. As the vegetation flourished, hunger no longer became a plague upon our people, and our numbers multiplied.

Single-handedly (or rather, single-*mindedly*) I transformed Terra-Mar into the metropolis that our ancestors had always hoped it would become.

And then the Neptuan immigrants came—emaciated people in their faded blue and orange robes, seeking an easier way of life. They docked their fleets of colossal quartz submarines outside our hatch, like schools of ghostly fish clustered at the reefs for safety.

The Terra-Marans welcomed them at first—space wasn't an issue with the multitude of empty pods throughout the metro. But then, more of the Neptuans came, crowding eagerly into our home. To reduce the risk of overpopulation, Ruben advised me to seal the hatch at the ground level and create a designated docking pod next to my own in my chosen locale of Zeta, so that I may personally oversee the entrance of immigrants into the metro and inform him of any overloads. I did this with strict determination, and soon, the amount of people entering Terra-Mar decreased. The metro's population stabilized just in time as the pods at each locale reached maximum capacity.

It only took one year for Terra-Mar to become completely reinvented, rebuilt, and enhanced. I was just seven years old.

As a token of my appreciation for Ruben's guidance, I secretly downloaded several files describing the science of optometry, and created a new pair of glasses for him that better suited his prescription. No longer did he have to squint in order to see.

Together, he and I stood—proud student, and even prouder teacher—outside the classroom of the top level, and gazed down at the bustling metro beneath us. Young children trickled to and fro on the bridges, greeting the new teachers that Ruben had trained, all of them looking plump and energetic. Among the gardens at the ground level stood the old quartz classroom, now simply a memorial for the old, challenging days of Terra-Mar.

If anyone addressed me as Alan at that point in my short life, I would no longer respond. I was the Creator, the child prodigy, the extraordinary imaginaire.

I was all-powerful.

CHAPTER 2

I was nine when Garrett and I became officially acquainted—or rather, *re*-acquainted. I hadn't seen him since Ruben exempted me from the classes all the other children went to so I could concentrate on creation. I was wandering toward the classroom from Zeta, looking curiously over the bridge railing at the jungle of pineapple, lime, and coconut trees beneath me.

In a clearing near the old quartz classroom, the quiet Terra-Maran boy knelt in the dirt, his black pants dusty up to his knees. His short hair was combed neatly forward over his olive forehead, and his forest-green eyes focused on the metal blocks he was meticulously stacking—*click, click, click*—into a tower. Sal and Belinda knelt across from him with their backs to me, engaged in conversation. Belinda's fiery-red strands now reached all the way down to her thighs.

On either side of them were two Neptuan immigrants I vaguely recognized—a tan-skinned boy named Chad and a girl named Joy who liked to tie her hair into a bouncy blonde ponytail above her head. The five of them smiled as they helped Garrett construct his block building.

The doors of the obsidian classroom near me swung open, and out streamed the children. As they bounded past me on the bridge, they greeted with a cheerful, "Hello, Creator!" or "Thank you for everything you give us, Creator!"

Waving absentmindedly to them, I kept my focus on the five children in the clearing. I was fascinated that, despite all the comforts I had imagined for them, they were still kneeling in the dirt and building with their hands instead of sitting in desks and designing 3-D models on their sleek new tablets. They even seemed like they were having *fun*.

With an illustrious swish of her flaming hair, Belinda peered over her shoulder, her crystal-blue eyes locking onto mine in recognition. Rising, she patted dust off her pants and trotted in my direction.

"Hey, Alan," she called. "Do you want to come down and build with us?"

My mind churned and my cheeks warmed with embarrassment. Belinda was the first person in a long time to call me by my real name. Hearing that made me feel less than what I was.

I hated being just... Alan. I hated when people called me that.

Flaring my freckled nose, I replied disdainfully, "You mean with my *hands*?"

Belinda paused, her grin curling downward into a frown. Behind her, the other children seemed to sense a disturbance and stopped their stacking to look in her direction.

The red-haired girl crossed her arms over her chest. "Well, if you're too busy to build with us non-imaginatives, you could just *say so!* No need to be *arrogant* about it!"

With a rueful *hmph*, she marched back to her posse, head held high and defiant.

I gaped. How dare she speak to me like that? I was the Creator, after all. I deserved her respect. Nothing in the grand metropolis of Terra-Mar would be here if it weren't for me. How could she be so rude?

I thought about running all the way to the top level, where Ruben was training a handful of new teachers, and telling him about the insult I'd just endured. But then I realized that Belinda had revealed something about myself I'd never noticed before—a divide between myself and the rest of the Terra-Marans.

Had my creating ability made me too almighty to associate with those less imaginative than myself? With those who couldn't create at all?

In a panic, I dashed down the steps to the ground level, across a winding trail leading through the kale. Approaching the clearing, I heard snippets of their conversation.

"It was supposed to be four hundred forty-three meters from the base to the antenna," Joy said, sliding the metal block in her hand into a gap at the center of the third layer.

"Wow, that's amazing!" Chad replied. "Buildings that tall... Not even Terra-Mar is like that!"

"I'm sure we *could* be," Garrett said timidly, a reserved smile on his face as he gathered an armful of blocks from a pile behind him. "At the rate we're going, we could be as tall as the buildings of the past."

"That's true," Sal nodded. "The levels here were built because our standard of living improved, which was what happened in the city of New York right before everyone got depressed during the Great Depression. But anyway, maybe one day, if more Neptuans come in, we could build our entire metro to be as tall as that building."

Noticing my arrival, the group tensed and turned their eyes in my direction—all except Belinda, that is. Suddenly, I felt self-conscious again, like the day of my first creation. I stared back at them, not knowing what to say.

With a shy nod, Joy greeted me, "Creator."

"Hi Creator," Chad and Sal said together. Their lips stretched into forced smiles.

"Hello, Creator," Garrett said, his eyes fixing onto mine for a moment before darting quickly away.

Finally I looked to Belinda, expecting her to acknowledge me, but her back remained stubbornly turned.

Hesitantly, I stepped between her and Sal (who shifted aside to allow me more space) and lowered myself to the ground, gulping back disgust when my palms pressed against the dirt. It had been a long time since I last knelt in the soil, and to dirty my pants like this now was appalling.

Still looking in Belinda's direction, I noticed the glowing screen of the tablet by her side. It displayed the image of a building I'd seen a few times while Ruben was teaching me about the old world metros. I tried to recall the name of it as I admired its stately design, the majestic reflectiveness of its roof as its antenna scraped the endless blue expanse above it.

That blue expanse... what was it called again?

The sky, I remembered dreamily, momentarily lost in the image's wonder. *It's so beautiful. How awesome would it be if I could actually see it for myself? Does it even still exist?*

When Belinda finally turned to look at me, I was wearing a dazed expression, my eyes locked on the tablet.

She looked from my face to the computer and said lightly, "We're building a miniature replica of the Empire State Building." As she continued, her expression softened. "It was originally the tallest building that people built in the past, before a bunch of newer buildings took that title."

Before I could control my stupid mouth, I scoffed, "You don't have enough blocks to build something as big as that, not even as a replica."

A wave of shame crashed into me as the red-headed girl's expression hardened once more into a glare. The other children held their breaths.

"Well, that's why you'll *create* more blocks when we run out, right?" Belinda snapped. "I mean, that's what you do after all, isn't it? You *create*."

I opened my mouth tentatively, only to close it again. She was right. I was the Creator. I could bring anything into existence, as long as I understood how it worked, what it was made of, and its purpose.

Why hadn't I thought of that before?

I stared down at my dusty hands, which I'd been clutching embarrassedly in my lap. In front of me, the other four children were silent, shocked to see me in such a humiliated state.

Seeing that she'd put me in my place, Belinda picked up her tablet and turned back to her friends as if I wasn't even there.

"I was thinking that we could build it in three separate sections," she proposed briskly. "And then when they're done we can connect them to make the complete model."

"Good idea, Belinda!" Joy gushed, eager to lighten the heavy mood.

"We can finish the base today, then start the middle tomorrow after our morning class," Chad joined in brightly.

The blocks clicked away as the five children went back to their building, occasionally glancing at me to gauge my mood. I listened to them talk about topics that I knew tremendously well—electrical engineering, computer science, welding—but couldn't bring myself to add one word to their conversation. These children were practically finishing each other's sentence, like separate parts of one well-oiled machine.

And I just didn't fit into that.

Hesitantly, I reached for the closest block and wrapped my fingers around it. The coolness of the metal reminded me of Terra-Mar's difficult early years, when we slept in the dirt and lived everyday with bellies that were only half-full. I lifted the block carefully off the ground, and placed it—*click*—on the formation next to Belinda's. After a moment, I reached for another block near Sal and set it—*click* —next to my first one. The two watched me with intrigue as I continued stacking blocks—*click, click, click*—until the supply was extinguished.

I sat back and admired my creation. It was the first I'd ever made with my hands. But I could feel the other children's eyes on me, waiting expectantly. I knew exactly what they wanted, so without question, I closed my eyes and held my palms over the dirt, imagining the glint of metal and the feel of its sleek surface in my hands.

The familiar warming sensation rippled over the surface of my skin, and when I opened my eyes again, there was a surplus of blocks piled haphazardly around us. The children pounced on them happily, wasting no time in beginning the fourth layer of the formation.

For the first time since I'd sat down, they smiled—even the steel-willed Belinda.

Together, the six of us quickly finished the model's foundation and proceeded on to the middle section, grinning all the while and exchanging short, encouraging words. As we built, I was constantly reminded that I could've easily created this replica on my own, but for the first time in a long time, I wasn't alone.

And I realized that I missed the company.

"Well, look at this," said a familiar drawl from behind me.

Dropping the blocks, I spun around to see Ruben approaching on the winding path from the stairs, his trusty tablet cradled under his arm.

Unidentifiable panic swept over me, and I immediately shifted away from the other children. My teacher, who had always kept a keen eye on me, would surely find it shameful that I was kneeling in the dirt like a lowly gardener after he'd taught me to create so many fine things.

After all, Ruben hadn't just taught me how to create. He'd trained me to behave better than this—to sit in chairs, type on a screen, and build things with my mind instead of dirtying my hands.

He must have been thoroughly disappointed with me.

But to my relief, a smile stretched across his sallow face.

"Ruben!" Belinda said brightly in greeting. The rest of the children joined in welcoming him.

The teacher tucked his tablet closer to him and lowered himself to one knee. "Do you know how hard it is to get Builders to work together toward one common goal?" Ruben mused. "And yet here you all are, cooperating with such perfect harmony. What, may I ask, are you building?"

"A model of the Empire State Building!" Joy answered, grinning excitedly over the blocks, which had now reached the height of her chin.

"Oh?" Ruben asked shortly—his way of coaxing his students to elaborate.

"Yeah," Chad affirmed. He reached over for Belinda's tablet and held the screen up to Ruben, pointing to the image of the building. "It measured over four hundred meters from the bottom to the antenna."

"And we're going to build it in three stages from today to the day after tomorrow," Sal added proudly.

"The Creator is going to help us every block of the way, isn't he?" Belinda said pointedly, looking over at me with hopeful eyes.

Glancing sheepishly at Ruben, I saw that he was still smiling, but his tightened grip around his tablet suggested otherwise.

"Well, it's always good to see the Creator working with his fellow classmates," my teacher said stiffly. "After all, he created everything in Terra-Mar for you. Aren't you grateful for everything he's done?"

"Oh, yes, we are!" Chad said hastily, lowering Belinda's tablet onto his lap.

"We are *very* grateful!" Sal and Joy agreed, nodding far too enthusiastically.

"Of course," Belinda said coolly with a pat on my shoulder. "We're all in his debt."

Scanning the faces of my companions, I didn't know how to feel. I wanted to tell them that it was alright to disagree with Ruben, but then again, he wasn't wrong. I *had* created everything here, something I would never have been able to do without Ruben.

With a light chuckle, Ruben said, "Well, how would you like it if I made you all part of a *special project* to help the Creator build something very important for our metro? You'll be exempt from all your regular classes, studying with me and the Creator instead. Would you like that?"

I could practically feel the neurons racing through my companions' brains as they considered this rare opportunity. Ruben was normally so protective of me—it was the reason I'd never spent any time with them before.

But Belinda didn't need time to think it over. "Yes, we would!" she answered immediately.

"That would be amazing!" Chad agreed.

"Please let us help!" Sal and Garrett said.

My companions broke into a frenzy of excitement as Ruben rose to his feet, clearly brimming with contentment. While the five children continued to unleash their storm of gratitude, he gently patted the dust off his pants and turned back toward the stairs.

"Thank you so much for including us!" Belinda called, rising to wave at him.

"Yes," Garrett agreed fanatically, jumping to his feet as well. "Thank you for—"

But before he could finish, an unexpected *ka-lack* interrupted him. I spun around to see Garrett tumbling face-first into the replica, sending metal blocks skittering across the dirt in every direction. The other children gaped as the boy struggled clumsily to his feet—grabbing at the blocks to keep his balance, but then falling onto his face once again.

"Our replica!" Belinda gasped.

"Are you alright?" Joy asked, grabbing Garrett's arm while Sal rounded behind him to grab the other. Together, they pulled him up to his feet and patted the dirt off his clothes.

"Yeah, I just tripped," the shy boy sighed, finally finding his footing. When he met my gaze, a terrified expression crossed his face and his eyes darted quickly away.

Confused, I turned back in Ruben's direction. My teacher had stopped mid-pace at the disturbance, his lips twisting and his shaggy eyebrows narrowed in what looked like fury.

Why is Ruben so mad at Garrett? I wondered, looking back at the boy who tripped.

It was just an accident.

The others noticed this also, and grew instantly silent, gazing back and forth between the teacher and the guilt-ridden boy.

For a few awkward seconds, Ruben continued to glare at Garrett, gripping his tablet with white knuckles. And then, without explanation, he turned and proceeded wordlessly back to the stairs, leaving us to stare after him in confusion.

Above us, the metro buzzed happily on, as if nothing strange was happening down here at the bottom of the world.

CHAPTER 3

That night, I lied awake in my bed, my thoughts troubled by what happened with Garrett earlier that afternoon. I tossed and turned in the dark, trying and failing to fall asleep. Finally surrendering to my overactive consciousness, I sat up—the fluorescent light bulbs activating above me—and planted my feet on the cold, iron floor.

I stared across my pod at the digital clock on my desk (the glowing red numbers read 21:20) and then at the baseball, my very first creation. Walking over to the desk, I picked the ball up and turned it over in my hands, my thoughts mulling.

Suddenly, I had an idea.

I dashed over to the foot of my bed and pulled my clothes on from the heap. Trotting to my door, I inched it open to peek outside at my locale, which was desolate at this late an hour.

I crouched to my knees and cupped my hands above a gap in the grated platform, imagining an aluminum can forming above it. When it appeared, I envisioned a piece of twine—no thicker than two or three millimeters—extending out of the can and snaking down through the gap toward Gamma, then connecting to the bottom of another aluminum can through a gap located right outside Garrett's door.

I tugged on the can a few times to wake Garrett up, hoping the noise would be enough to shake him from his slumber. Through the aluminum, I could hear the soft *clink, clink, clink* as the other can knocked against Garrett's pod. A moment later, my tug was returned and the boy's soft voice came filtering through the wire.

"Hello?" he asked uncertainly, his voice vibrating up from my can.

"Garrett, it's me!" I whispered, excited that my knowledge of primitive telephones was accurate.

"Creator?" he replied, astonished.

No, I thought. That name didn't seem right coming from him. He didn't need another authority figure, he needed a friend. *I'm not the Creator right now, I'm just me.*

"No, it's me, *Alan*. Were you sleeping?"

A pause.

"No."

"Good!" I said eagerly. "In that case, we can play *baseball*!"

"Now?" Garrett gasped, struggling to keep his volume down. "But it's so late..."

"Just meet me on the ground level in ten minutes," I said shortly, already dropping the can to push myself up to my feet.

"But...," he began. A dribble of stammers vibrated out of the can, as I rose, but I didn't wait to hear his excuses. I snatched the baseball from my desk and bolted out of the door, speeding off toward the top of the stairs.

A little more than ten minutes later, I arrived at the ground level to find Garrett already standing in the clearing where we and the other children had gathered that afternoon. The blocks had since been cleared away—stored up in the classroom of the lowest level for a more promising day of stacking.

The boy slouched with his hands stuffed in his pockets, staring at his dirty shoes. But hearing me trotting toward him, he straightened up.

"I don't know how to play baseball, Crea—I mean, Alan," he said.

"Well, we're not going to play an actual game. We'd need more people, and an actual baseball diamond, but what we *could* play with just two people is something called *catch*."

"Catch?" Garrett asked, and I nodded.

"It's really easy." I tossed the ball in the air and caught it coolly in my hands to demonstrate. "Two people stand a few feet from each other and throw the baseball back and forth. Usually they wear baseball mitts so they can catch the ball more easily."

"I don't know," Garrett sighed reluctantly. "It sounds kind of mundane."

"Catch is *not* mundane!" I answered defensively. "It's the way people got along in the past, before our fall from the stars. Whole friendships have been forged on this game. It's anything *but* mundane."

The boy's lips twisted nervously, so I closed my eyes and gathered my thoughts. I imagined the stiff feeling of leather wrapping around my hands, making an oversized glove.

When I opened my eyes, I smiled down at two leather baseball mitts in my hands. I looked up at Garrett and felt a wave of pride seeing his chin drop down in awe.

"Wow," he exhaled, his green eyes wide with amazement. "It never gets old to watch you create, especially up close like this."

My lips pulled up in a contented smile and I held up both of the mitts. "Oh, oops, I created opposing mitts by mistake. You're not left-handed, are you? I can just create another one—"

"Actually, I am," he answered quickly.

"And I'm right-handed."

We grinned simultaneously.

"Here," I said cheerfully, handing him his mitt. "This game is really simple. I'll throw the ball to you, and you catch it in your mitt. Then you throw the ball back to me, and I'll catch it in my mitt."

Garrett's forehead wrinkled anxiously as he backed to the edge of the clearing, stopping before a grove of lime trees. I stuffed my hand into my mitt and pressed the ball inside, holding them both against my chest.

"Ready?" I called as quietly as I could.

Extending his mitted hand out in front of him, the timid boy murmured, "Uh huh."

Shifting my weight to one side, I lifted my left leg as I'd seen pitchers do in videos and swung my arm backward before pitching the ball to Garrett.

Unsure of how to react, Garrett twisted awkwardly, missing the baseball with his glove only to catch it with his belly. He plopped onto the dirt with an *oof!* and hugged himself in pain.

"Catch it, Garrett, catch it!" I instructed impatiently, waving my mitt at him. "Don't just let it hit you."

"I need to get used to the technique, that's all," he grunted, pushing himself laboriously to his feet.

"Alright, alright," I sighed, walking around in circles as I waited for him to regain his bearings. When he was ready, I looked back at him and said, "Now, *you* throw the ball to *me*."

Huffing, Garrett bent forward to retrieve the ball, then straightened himself to mirror my posture. He tossed it weakly, sending the ball spinning up into the air before falling back down at a leisurely pace.

Before the ball could hit the dirt, I dove forward and caught it, only to land in a heap of dust with a cry of annoyance.

"Was that a bad throw?" Garrett asked worriedly.

"No, it was *great,*" I lied, and clambered to my feet. "If we were playing a real game, you might've even scored a point for your team."

Even though it was false encouragement, the boy smiled.

"Now this time, make sure to keep your eyes on the ball. Prepare to catch it before it reaches you. Understand?"

Garrett nodded and held his mitt out in front of him again.

This time, I thrust the ball straight toward the boy's chest, and he snatched it out of the air.

"You got it!" I cheered, a little louder than I'd intended.

Opening his mitt, Garrett gazed proudly upon his conquest, then excitedly prepared to throw the ball back to me.

For the next ten minutes or so, we went about our game, growing accustomed to each other's pitching habits.

"Hey, Alan," Garrett began curiously, mid-pitch. "How come you never played catch with Ruben?"

"I've always wanted to," I replied, seizing the ball out of the air. "But I figured he'd think it was mundane."

Garrett's face colored in embarrassment as he remembered his earlier comment, and he let the conversation drop.

After a few more throws, I spoke again.

"Do you remember that book we were reading in Ruben's class a long time ago? Back when we were six?"

"'Shoeless Joe'," he confirmed. "How could I forget it? We were reading it when you made your first creation." He looked at the baseball in admiration before tossing it into the air again.

"Do you remember that line that went, 'If you build it, he will come'? Why do you think he chose those words?"

Garrett shrugged. "Because he wanted to meet the baseball player, Shoeless Joe Jackson. He built the baseball field so that Shoeless Joe Jackson would go to it."

"Do you think—" I began pensively, catching the ball in my mitt. "Do you think that if I made Terra-Mar look like the great cities of the past, that someone would come to it, too? The way Shoeless Joe Jackson went to Kinsella's field?"

Garrett paused as he thought about this.

"Who'd come down here to Terra-Mar? Aren't we and the Neptuans the last human beings in the universe?"

I blinked hard and threw the ball back to him. "I don't know. Maybe someone from the surface? Or even the stars?"

"The surface?" Garrett asked, eyeing me incredulously. "The stars? Alan, there's nothing left for us up there. Not on Earth, and not in the rest of this galaxy."

My gaze dropped to the ground and I lowered my catching arm, lost in my own thoughts. Garrett must have noticed because he didn't throw the ball back in my direction until I met his eye again.

"I guess I just wonder why I'm doing all this," I said softly. "Learning new things with Ruben, enhancing the metro, making sure everyone is happy and comfortable here—I know that being the Creator means I have a duty to prolong the future generations of Terra-Mar, but there must be something out there for me, too."

Garrett didn't respond, but simply threw the ball underhanded to me.

For the next few minutes, we played in silence, pitching and catching the ball in smooth synchronicity.

"Sorry about what happened with the blocks today," I said suddenly.

"It's alright." Garrett kept his eye on the ball as it left my hand. "I was just really excited to help you with that special project and I wasn't looking at where I was stepping."

If you're still even part of it, I thought. *Now that you made Ruben angry.*

Feeling guilty for thinking this, I forced a grin and turned my attention to the ball Garrett was tossing to me.

"It must be great to be able to build with your imagination, though," Garrett said as I caught the ball easily.

I hesitated, making sure to keep my tone neutral. "Yeah, well, I'm glad everyone's happy with what I do."

"I'm probably not the best builder here, but I'm really proud to be one of the first people to know you before the Neptuans came. They say that Terra-Mar is a really special place because we have a Creator, and Neptua doesn't. Chad and Joy told me that they were still building with their hands before they heard about you on their radio. With you here, we're all living better lives, and who knows what other wonders you'll create for us in the future."

"Yeah, I guess..." I said sadly, but my companion didn't seem to notice my tone.

My next pitch came awkwardly, and I released the ball before I was ready. It bounced out of my palm and soared into the air in a lopsided bell curve.

Garrett dove forward to catch the ball, landing in a cloud of dust just as the ball dropped into the palm of the leather.

"Whoa, are you alright?" I ran over to him and bent down, feeling even guiltier now that I made him fall. "Sorry, that was a terrible throw."

"I'm fine," Garrett chuckled, taking my hand and regaining his footing. "If you'd done that in the past, you might've even scored a point for your team."

I smirked, then backed up again and held my hand and mitt out in preparation for his next pitch.

"Ready?" he asked, assuming his pitching stance. "Not dazing out again?"

"I'm wide awake and conscious, thank you," I laughed.

Swinging his arm in a circle, Garrett thrust the ball in my direction, sending it shooting toward me in a rapid blur. Shocked at the speed, I jumped out of the way just in time for it to whistle past my ears. It sliced through some leaves on the lime tree behind me and struck the gridded metal beneath the enclosure with a powerful *pong!*

The sound echoed loudly throughout the metro, and soon, startled voices emerged from the locales above.

"Whoa, Garrett, what was that?!" I asked, scurrying beneath the shade of the lime tree.

"I have no idea!" he responded, grinning.

Looking up, we watched as people in pajamas peeked out from above the bridge railings.

"Did you hear that?" a woman asked.

"The enclosure is breaking!" an old man declared in fright.

"No, it's not!" a younger man scolded back. "Don't say things like that! The enclosure is indestructible!"

"Where's the Creator? He'll fix the enclosure for us!"

"I just told you that the enclosure isn't breaking! Stop scaring everyone for no reason!"

After a brief argument between the two cranky Terra-Marans, everyone finally concluded that the enclosure was, indeed, not breaking, and that everyone was safe. Little by little, the people retired peacefully back to their pods, and the metro returned to silence.

Climbing out from beneath the leafy branches, Garrett and I whispered about the clueless Terra-Marans above, giggling at their fright. After we'd retrieved the fallen baseball, we decided it was time to head back.

"Thanks for teaching me this game, Alan," Garrett said, removing his mitt and brushing the dust off his clothes. "And for making me feel better about the blocks."

"You're welcome," I said with a shrug. "By the way, you should disconnect the twine from the can outside your door. Nobody can find out that we weren't in our pods tonight."

"I'll do that."

With a mischievous grin, the not-so-timid boy jogged off toward Gamma while I dashed in the opposite direction toward Zeta.

Reaching the deserted bridge at the top level, I leaned against the railings to look back down at the ground level, which now appeared to be nothing more than a sprawling circle of dirt and vegetation.

I realized that nothing I'd done thus far—saving the Terra-Marans' lives, gaining new and fascinating knowledge from Ruben, developing my creation abilities—had made me feel as satisfied as playing catch with Garrett.

For once in my short life, I felt like the boy I was.

He's interesting, alright, I thought of Garrett, gazing over in the direction of Gamma. *Whether or not he's still part of Ruben's special project, I'll make sure to visit him after classes sometime.*

Before returning to my own pod, I glanced over the railings one more time to examine the spot where the ball had struck the gridded metal. To my astonishment, I found a small dent there.

That's impossible! I thought, tilting my head in bafflement. *I created Terra-Mar to be completely indestructible. How could the simple throw of a baseball cause any damage to the infrastructure, even a minor one like this?*

But fatigue overtook my thoughts, and with a yawn I turned back to my pod, bending down to disconnect the aluminum can from the twine before stepping sleepily inside.

CHAPTER 4

One week after that night, Ruben instructed me to create a laboratory beneath the metro where my companions and I would undertake the "special project." So I set to work imagining a stainless steel shaft that extended one mile down beneath the ground level. At the bottom of the shaft, I envisioned a large room of high ceilings and sleek white floor tiles that spanned the ground level's area. I filled the room with a myriad of tools and building materials, then lined the ceiling with the same fluorescent light bulbs that were hung throughout the enclosure.

The day after this was done, Ruben and I crowded into the rudimentary elevator I'd made to reach the lower level—an electric pulley hidden behind the lime trees—and descended to the laboratory, the gears producing a soft churning as we went.

"This project must be kept top secret," my teacher advised, shifting away to allow me more space. "No one other than those involved are to know about this, not even your parents."

Crossing my arms over my chest, I nodded shortly. The ground that had been beneath us a moment ago slowly rose up past our heads and shrouded us in darkness.

A few minutes later, we arrived in the expansive laboratory to find Belinda, Chad, Sal, and Joy waiting eagerly, all standing next to each other in a neat line. Behind them, a white control panel curved outward in a semicircle around the pile of tools I'd created, all of them gleaming sleekly beneath the lights like netted fish. As my teacher and I descended further, I saw that Garrett stood slightly apart from the other children, all the way on the left of the line. A twinge of delight struck me.

He's here! I thought as the boy's forest-green eyes met mine with anticipation. I guess Ruben wasn't mad at him after all.

When the elevator settled, the children rushed up to us, brimming with excitement. I couldn't help but notice the trail of dirt around their feet, tracked in from the garden above and starkly offset by the sterile white tiles.

"Amazing laboratory, Alan!" Belinda gushed, her eyes sparkling.

"Yeah, great creation, Alan," Chad agreed. He punched me playfully in the shoulder as if that were normal.

"Alan, It's really amaz—" Garrett began, but Ruben cut him off.

"Alan is nothing less than phenomenal, as always." He swept briskly between me and Garrett on his way to the control panel, which blinked to life with the wave of his hand. "But now that this lab is actually built, we need to get to work."

While the others turned toward Ruben, Garrett leaned into me and whispered, "This lab is the best place in the world."

The corner of my mouth pulled up in an instinctual smile.

Ruben hunched over the control panel and tapped through the icons, projecting a series of holographic lights above the tools. They whirled and tumbled in a rainbow of colors before separating into floating spheres of various sizes. The one at the center was the biggest, and was particularly vibrant, like a ball of fire.

The solar system, I thought, observing some of the smallest spheres orbiting around the larger ones. Ruben was showing us our universe, though at what point in time, I didn't know.

"Traditionally, builders are self-minded individuals who prefer to work alone to achieve their goals." Ruben gazed intently at the holograms in front of him. "But you are all here today because you are a rare group of builders whose skills and personalities complement one another. This project can only be accomplished through cooperation and patience—it is a very challenging feat."

My companions exchanged looks, reveling in the honor of working so closely with Terra-Mar's Creator.

And I was proud of them, too.

Pressing his fingers on the screen, our teacher zoomed in to focus on one of the spheres in the hologram—the fourth from the sun. Its crystalline outer crust, illuminated by a jewel-like mirage of electric lights, glimmered atop the rusty brown terrain.

The Mars colony, I recognized. That was where the ancestors of Terra-Mar and Neptua came from.

"Never forget that humanity fell from the stars," Ruben said, his voice emboldening with the weight of his words. "We didn't sprout from the earth like worms. We were once ingenious beings that dominated this solar system—*ruled* it like gods. We bent it to our will, transforming otherwise hostile and unsuitable environments into habitats where we thrived and prospered. We made our home among the stars, and expanded across the galaxy."

A cloud of gray suddenly smoldered out from the glimmering expanse, sending a barrage of reflective debris floating out past the thin atmosphere.

Ruben fell silent while the rest of us waited for the cloud to settle. It never did.

"But then, people destroyed our homes—*their own* homes." His voice sharpened venomously. "They resisted invention and innovation, preferring to live in the dark ages instead."

On the hologram, a stream of glowing tear-drop objects flew out of the cloud, hovering momentarily above the remains of their glimmering origins before gliding toward the burning sun like tadpoles.

Around me, my companions shifted uncomfortably.

We've all heard the story of the Mars colony's destruction, I thought with a bit of annoyance. *What is Ruben trying to prove?*

Ruben lifted his hand gently from the screen and the hologram zoomed out from Mars, past the asteroid belt separating Jupiter from the inner planets. We watched as the space crafts drifted away into the distance, slowly being replaced by a set of reflective objects that emerged around the edges of the hologram. They were the crystalline remnants of space crafts, and among them floated disembodied limbs—the horrific remains of people frozen in the negative-degree temperature of deep space. My companions and I gasped.

We are the last human survivors after all, I thought morbidly. *There was no one left from the other colonies.*

"The people who destroyed the innovations of the past could not fathom the importance of what their more inventive counterparts were doing." Ruben's voice now lowered to a hiss. "Because of their incompetence, they destroyed an entire way of life—one that once brought prosperity to all of humanity. It was the only hope we had after the earth failed to protect us."

The hologram zoomed back in, through the asteroid belt and gray cloud of Mars, past the fleet of sparkling space crafts, and finally stopped at a gargantuan blue planet—the third sphere from the sun.

Earth.

We watched as the hologram penetrated the planet's atmosphere, piercing through the fluffy gray vapors of the sky and halting above an endless rippling surface of mysterious blue.

The ocean, formed by long-ago ice that used to dominate the planet's poles.

But it wasn't the blue of the rippling surface that held my attention. It was the blue of the sky above—so light and sublime.

While my teacher lectured on about humanity's tragic fall from the stars, I stared at the soft white clouds that stretched across the light blue sky, like deep-sea porpoises sailing through a lazy ocean current.

The sky, I thought wondrously, slipping into one of my dazes again. *It must be beautiful up there, above the surface. If I could only see it with my own eyes...*

Would Ruben ever let me do that?

In a split-second, the innocent light blue was marred by a searing flash of flaming orange as the Martian space crafts burned through the air and splashed into the rippling water.

Our disgraced return to the earth, I thought bitterly as the hologram finally faded to the artificial light of the laboratory.

There was a tense silence as the icons on the screen slowly winked to black. Beside me, my companions inhaled labored breaths—we'd learned about the harrowing history of our metro time and again, but we'd never truly experienced it like that.

"They should have been rounded up and executed like the criminals they were," Ruben spat, the loathing in his voice tearing through the silence. He balled his fists. "Because of them, we are damned to the bottom of this miserable hellhole called the ocean. Because of them, humanity is now trapped under the dirty, grimy foot of the most despicable place in the universe, and there's nothing we can do about it. Not even with the millennia of knowledge that we've compiled in the prison of this harsh and abominable reality."

With a sudden *thunk,* Ruben slammed his fists onto the panel, making the group of us jump.

No one dared to move until he straightened again. He moved wearily, as if all his energy had been sucked out by this strange, upsetting lesson.

"As you can see, the truth about all of us is pretty grim." Ruben sighed tragically, turning away from us. "We may seem like we're thriving in Terra-Mar, but humanity is only hanging on by a thread. Even if we continue receiving immigrants from Neptua, there is nothing here for us to grow as a civilization. The only thing we can achieve is a bigger enclosure that's still stuck at the bottom of this never-ending ocean. There is nowhere left for us to go."

"Then what are we supposed to do?" Belinda asked in a small, scared voice. "If humanity is failing in Terra-Mar, even with all of Alan's creations, what can we possibly build to stop it from continuing?"

Suddenly Ruben whipped around, an unexpected smile on his face. It was more frightening than reassuring.

"My dear Belinda," he said, his tone returning to its familiar evenness. "We need to build something to stop our homes in the stars from ever being destroyed. We need to erase our fall from history, and regain our rightful place in the heavens."

The room grew so quiet that I was sure my companions had stopped breathing.

I met Ruben's eyes with incredulity. "You want us to build a time machine."

His smile stretched even wider. "Exactly."

Every jaw in the room dropped open in confusion. Had Ruben gone crazy? A *time machine?* It never existed in the past—what made him think we could make one now?

I stared down at the sleek tiles and ran one hand concernedly through my hair. My head began to pulse with the old familiar feeling of a headache—something I hadn't experienced for years. If no one could teach me how a time machine worked, or what it was made of, I simply couldn't create it. It was absolutely impossible.

Turning coolly back to the control panel, our teacher tapped on some of the icons to produce a plethora of holographic scripts. A flurry of equations, symbols, and characters floated before us.

"Time has been represented throughout human history in many different ideals— the Greek god Kronos, aging, and the advancement of future societies. For this project, you all need to help the Creator find the perfect avatar to model the machine's functionality. Once he can formulate an applicable concept of time, it'll be much easier for him to-"

"What are you talking about?" I exclaimed, throwing my hands up wildly. "Time isn't something I can just pluck out of the air and replicate. It's not something I can touch, or see, or smell. Time is much bigger than me—it's out of my control!"

My breath quickened and my heart pounded in my chest. There, I said it: *it's out of my control.* For three whole years, I had raised Terra-Mar from the ocean floor using nothing but my knowledge of the past and my own imagination. I'd never once thought that there would be an invention for which I had no basis of reference.

All at once, I felt useless. Pitifully, and utterly useless.

But Ruben wasn't dissuaded.

"It may seem out of your control now," he said. "But you'll learn how time works. Slowly, you'll understand the intricacies of space and relatively, and figure out how to bring this time machine into existence."

"No, I can't, I..." My mouth turned to cotton, and I moved away from my teacher. Ruben wasn't willing to budge on this, even though it was futile. Why couldn't he see that it was futile?

Stepping further from the group, I bent down and clutched my head. The curved white walls of the laboratory were spinning around me.

This was all too much. I simply could not create a time machine.

I hardly heard the sound of his footsteps as Ruben approached and dropped one hand on my shoulder.

"You *can* do it, Alan," he said, kneeling in front of me. He leaned in close enough for me to see every wrinkle and crease in his skin. "Building this time machine is not simply for us, but for our ancestors from Mars, and the people of the other colonies. When we succeed, no one here will ever know the hardships of this life under the ocean. Do this now and you will never again be asked to carry the weight of humanity's future. You will no longer have to be the Creator, because there will no longer be a need for one. We will all be up on Mars, enjoying the comforts of the past. I beg of you, Alan, at least try. You will regret it forever if you don't."

When, I repeated in my mind. *He said "when" we succeed, as if he already knows that I'll agree. Or maybe he's just being hopeful.*

I stared back at Ruben, not knowing how to sway his unwavering conviction. He was just so confident that I'd be able to do it, even though it was impossible.

"What will happen to us when you die, Creator?" Belinda asked softly. I looked over to see all of my peers wearing matching concerned expressions. "In seventy or eighty years, what will happen to the future generations of Terra-Mar when you—" she lowered her eyes, "pass on? If our numbers continue to grow, and you're no longer with us, who will expand the enclosure to accommodate for the increasing population? Who will have the power to help us live down here in the bottom of the sea?"

No one, I concluded. *I am the sole Creator of Terra-Mar—of this whole universe. If I'm not here to help the metro, no one will be.*

In my peripheral vision, I saw Chad step forward past Belinda, the light of the lab brightening his tanned skin to a pale gold.

"Belinda is right," he said. "We can't survive without you. Our only option is to make it so we never needed a Creator in the first place."

I looked over at my companions, who were nodding to each other in agreement. When I caught sight of Garrett, his forest-green eyes were pleading.

"Your friends need you to do this," Ruben said.

My friends, I thought, looking directly at Garrett. *I only have one friend.*

And just like that, the decision was made.

CHAPTER 5

Humanity may have fallen from the stars, but it evolved from the earth.

For the next two years, my friends and I scourged the lab's infinite database for any information that would help us achieve our goal, projecting textbook scripts, images, and videos onto the hologram in a dizzying array.

In order to understand the concept of time, we first had to learn how it was understood by the earliest human civilizations — the Romans, Greeks, Chinese, Mayans — and how their various calendars overlapped. We racked our brains trying to find the reasoning behind time's various measurements — years, months, weeks, all the way down to nano-seconds. Then we looked further, to the use of solar cycles, lunar cycles, and natural events like rains, floods, the flowering of trees, and the breeding cycles of animals. We also examined inventions that were used to measure the passage of time — hourglasses, sundials, pendulums, wristwatches, and ultimately, the digital clock.

We read until our eyes were sore and our heads ached, but we found nothing that could help us build a machine.

So we decided to change course and study topics that were less obvious: the major scientific theories of the past — Galileo's law of dynamics, Isaac Newton's findings on gravity, Albert Einstein's theory of relativity, Nikola Tesla's experiments with energy and electricity —anything that could even remotely elude to the role of time in human lives.

Again, we found nothing that could be of practical use.

At the end of those two mentally grueling years, we looked vastly different than when we started the project. Belinda had cut her hair to her shoulders, while Joy had grown hers to her lower back, and become fond of braiding it. They had both gotten taller than I and the other boys – and had also developed small breasts, which I admittedly peaked at on several occasions, when they were not looking. Sal's frame had thinned, reed-like, while Chad's midsection widened slightly from accumulated weight. Garrett's shoulders grew broader and stronger, and his personality emboldened along with it once he became more comfortable with all of us. As for me—well, I suppose I'd gained a couple of inches.

But as much as we'd developed physically, we were still just a bunch of eleven year olds milling around without a single clue about what we were doing. Two years down the line and we weren't any closer to building a time machine.

"Nothing!" Belinda cried angrily from behind the control panel, slapping her hands down on the screen. On the hologram in front of her, an image of an old Victorian grandfather clock flickered from the force. "Searching and searching for weeks on end, lying to my parents about going to class when I'm really buried down here like a worm, and for what? We've still got no answers on how to build this stupid machine!"

"What is the machine supposed to look like, anyway?" Sal wondered aloud, leaning his elbows over the back of a metal chair that I created. His head was buried in his hands, his short blonde hair sticking out in tufts between his fingers. "We've been focusing so much on understanding time, but we don't even know how to *picture* it."

Belinda peered impatiently over her shoulder at him. "Well, Sal, if you weren't just sitting around all the time whining about everything, maybe we would've established a design by now!"

"Hey!" Joy called defensively, the video recording of some fruit-eating chimpanzees playing in front of her. "Sal stayed up every night last week reading Kepler's manuscript on elliptical orbits. Don't say that he hasn't done anything for this project!"

Before Belinda could snap back at Joy, Chad held his hands up to silence them. "It doesn't matter who's been doing how much work. The important thing is that Alan understands time so he can create the machine."

Then, to me, he asked uncertainly, "You *are* beginning to understand it, right?"

My lips twisted hesitantly at a hologram in front of me, which showed Robert Boyle's notes on pressure and volumes in gases. "I'm sorry, but I don't think so. There're just so much information, and not enough explanations on how it all refers to time."

"I have an idea," Garrett said, stepping in front of the control panel where the pile of tools stood unused, a thin film of dust now covering them. "Why don't we try actually building the machine *before* finding the concept? That way, we can at least make some sort of progress."

"That doesn't make any sense," Belinda scoffed, crossing her arms over her chest.

Sal peered darkly at her. "It's better than coming up empty-handed like we have been for the past two years."

"Hey, look," I began, growing aggravated myself. "I know it's been a long time, but let's just concentrate on our research, and—"

"How can we build something if we don't know what it's supposed to look like?" Belinda snapped, ignoring me.

"Well, we don't see *you* coming up with any new ideas!" Joy challenged.

"Everyone, please."

"Belinda has sorted through more data in one hour than *you* have in one day!" Chad barked. "Don't judge her so quickly when you haven't done anything better!"

"We shouldn't compare ourselves—"

"Don't talk to Joy like that!" Sal yelled over at Chad, leaping up to his feet with balled fists.

"Everyone!" I shouted, finally losing my temper. "Stop arguing, and start working togeth—"

But before I could finish, Sal lunged for Chad, locking both hands around his neck and knocking him to the floor with a *thunk*. Belinda screamed as the boys started hitting each other, rolling across the tiles and punching as hard as they could.

In a flurry of panic, Garrett and I scurried toward the fistfight and tried to pull the boys apart, but only ended up receiving some sidelong blows ourselves. We stumbled back onto the floor, me holding the spot on my belly where I was elbowed and Garrett rubbing one side of his face, where he was haphazardly slapped.

Amidst all the confusion, nobody noticed the familiar scrape of the elevator as Ruben descended into the lab.

"What's going on?!" he bellowed, marching off the platform.

Chad and Sal promptly disconnected and rolled away from each other, wiping at the blood that streaked across their faces. Pointing an accusing finger, Chad said, "Sal's just been sitting on his butt, asking pointless questions and not doing any research!"

Glaring back with one swollen eye, Sal barked, "I wouldn't be asking questions if you and Belinda had already found the design for the machine!"

"At least I'm actually *doing* something," Belinda growled. "There just isn't anything to find!"

Garrett looked to me pleadingly, but I didn't know what to say. Neither of us did.

"Children, children," Ruben began exasperatedly, gripping each boy by the arm and pulling them to their feet. "Let me emphasize again the importance of finishing this time machine as soon as possible. The metro has been growing rapidly—there were ten new births just this past year, as well as talk of more immigrants from Neptua. Now, what solutions *have* you found?"

My friends stared at one another speechlessly as Garrett and I heaved ourselves up. Chad sniffed at a drop of blood dribbling from his nose.

Finally, Garrett stepped forward. "Well, I suggested that we start building the machine, even though we haven't found the concept."

Ruben's eyebrow twitched in annoyance, and he turned to the boy slowly, the shadow of a scowl on his sallow face.

Garrett continued shakily, "I just thought that actually building something would help us make sense of our research. We've only been using the database for the past two years, and we haven't found anything. But we have all these materials here, so why not try and visualize? Sometimes you don't understand something until you see it with your own eyes..."

He trailed off, dropping his arms to his sides in defeat. But to my surprise, my friends weren't ignoring him—they looked intrigued. They had actually listened to Garrett this time, and what he'd said made sense.

Start from the end, and then maneuvering our way back to the beginning—we'd thought it silly before, but with the frustration and physical pain we were causing each other by browsing aimlessly through endless masses of data, it suddenly didn't seem like such a bad idea.

I opened my mouth to agree, but Ruben beat me to the punch. "Absolutely not, you must find the concept first before building the machine. If you don't, mistakes are sure to—"

"But who knows how long that could take!" I answered defiantly. "It's been two years and we're no closer to understanding time than the day we started. You said it yourself—we need to build the machine as soon as possible. Maybe this way we can realize the concept along the way!"

"I'm the teacher, and I know what's best!" Ruben snapped, startling me so much that I jumped. His brows narrowed into a knife's edge, angrier than I'd ever seen him. "If you start building the machine now, you will make catastrophic, irreversible mistakes! Find the concept first, *then* build the machine."

"But—" I stammered.

"Find the concept first!"

And with that, Ruben swept back to the elevator, stomped onto the platform, and ascended back to the ground level.

....

That night, in the solace of the empty lab, Garrett and I sat cross-legged next to the pile of building materials. We sorted through the tools in preparation for building the time machine, the soft clinking of metal reverberating through the vast, lonely space.

"Well, *I* think your idea is great, Garrett," I said, attempting to match a handful of variously-sized screws to their proper holes in a metal sheet. "Ruben thinks there's only one way to do everything. But you're right—sometimes you have to create something to truly understand it. Trust me, I would know."

The boy nodded morosely at the tools in his lap.

For a few minutes, we worked quietly, sorting through the mismatched screws. I tried to come up with a pleasant topic to make Garrett feel better, but all I could think about was the tediousness of this hold project, so I held my tongue.

Running out of screws, I turned my back to Garrett to reach for more, only to hear a screeching metallic *crunch.* Spinning back around in alarm, I found Garrett holding a crumpled ball of metal where the sheet used to be.

"Whoa, what happened?" I gasped.

"Um, I don't know." He stared blankly down at the ruined material.

"Did you do that?"

A pause.

"N-no," Garret answered uncertainly.

My brows pulled together, noting his frightened expression. "Are you alright?"

After another worrying pause, Garrett said in a low tone, "Yeah, I think so," and set the crumpled metal down behind him, hiding it from view. He reached for a new sheet and sheepishly began matching screws.

But I couldn't ignore what had just happened. I sat with my hands in my lap, waiting patiently until Garrett was ready to continue.

"I don't think Ruben likes me," he finally said, still not meeting my eyes.

"Why do you think that?"

Garrett shrugged.

"Oh, you know, he doesn't think I can help you build the time machine. He doesn't think I can build *anything.* He's hated me ever since the day I fell into the blocks."

He dropped a screw into the hole of his current sheet, where it fit perfectly.

"He barely talks to me—he doesn't even *look* at me unless I make him angry. I don't know why he asked me to be a part of this project. I try to mention some of the things I've researched to him, but, you know, he always ignores me. He clearly thinks I'm useless, so why does he want me here?"

My gaze dropped back to my lap.

I knew why Ruben had included Garrett on this project. It didn't take much to see that our friendship was strong. But there was another, more important reason that Ruben didn't know about—Garrett made me feel balanced. Whenever I grew frustrated with the project, he calmed me down, and reassured me that I was capable of building the time machine, even if I couldn't do it right now. Whatever this timid boy was, he was definitely useful, and he made *me* feel useful. I was determined to do whatever it took to keep him with me.

....

The next day, Ruben descended into the lab to find me and my five friends all sitting with a metal sheet in our lap, working harmoniously to match the sheets of metal surrounding us with their appropriately sized screws.

"What in this deep, dark bottom of the universe are you all *doing?!*"

the teacher exclaimed frantically, stumbling off the platform and racing toward us.

I held up two fastened pieces of metal. "We're building a time machine."

"Well, I can see that!" Ruben scoffed, still waiting for me to provide an explanation that favored him. When I did not, he looked to Belinda, who was wrapping a strip of blue rubber around some frayed copper wires.

"We figured we'd try Garrett's idea," she said with a shrug. Beside her, the timid boy grinned up from a bouquet of frayed wires.

Ruben looked quickly from one student to the next, but no one else would meet his eyes. "Executing the plan with the opposite perspective," Joy said to the tools in her hands. "It's so crazy it might just work!"

She and Chad rose to their feet, lifting two fastened sheets between them.

Overwhelmed by our disobedience, Ruben trembled with pent-up fury. Instead of releasing it on us, though, he whipped back toward the elevator, his fists balled at his sides.

Stomping onto the platform, he looked up at the shaft impatiently, clearly dying to get out of there. But as the elevator slowly ascended, something caught his attention. He glanced to the corner of the room where Garrett's crumpled sheet of metal from last night sat abandoned, then looked back up at the shaft with a strange expression I couldn't identify.

Regardless, watching Ruben disappear into the ceiling gave me a twinge of satisfaction. My teacher had finally (albeit grudgingly) allowed me to do something that *I* wanted to do.

CHAPTER 6

My companions and I spent another two years trying to piece our materials into some sort of recognizable structure—fastening layers of metal together, coating copper wires with plastic, anything we could think of that might make sense. Still, we were no closer to finding an applicable concept of time.

By then, all of our thirteenth birthdays had come and gone. Belinda and Joy had both matured to intelligent, lean young women, and the boys had all hit their growth spurts. Garrett had become fond of jogging around the perimeter of the ground level every morning for exercise, and the results were evident. I had grown a few more inches too.

We became very close during that time, spending every waking moment in the lab, but we were still no close to discovering Ruben's mysterious concept with which to build his time machine.

Time. It was the greatest lesson that I'd never been able to learn. And yet, it was all around me.

I stood at the control panel, my wrists resting on the screen, and thought fleetingly about how small I'd been when this project began—the control panel had reached up to my chest back then. In front of me floated various holograms of ancient scripts written by the greatest philosophers of human history. I scrolled through them for the tenth time this week, hoping against hope to find any mention of time travel.

Behind me, Garrett, Sal, and Joy murmured to each other while trying to create some sort of thick pipe. To my right, Belinda hummed to herself, using art software to draw a digital angel fish blowing bubbles out of its mouth. To my left, Chad played a computer game that involved shooting virtual pebbles out of a digital slingshot, each shot sounding—*blip, blip, blip*—through the speakers in the control panel.

Bored, confused, and out of ideas, the six of us were nothing more than lonely adolescents killing time in an enormous room at the bottom of the ocean.

And then, as I continued scrolling through the scripts, I started to wonder. Was time really just a series of seconds and minutes, days and weeks? Just another mathematical figure expanding infinitely in exponential terms?

Or did time have a soul? An actual soul, with thoughts and feelings?

What if time wasn't a concept at all, but an entity?

A living, breathing thing.

And what if in order to control it, I had to feel what it felt and think what it thought?

What if I had to *become* time?

"I think I figured it out..." I mumbled quietly, beginning to understand. Behind me, the clicks and clangs of the metal sheets quieted, and the beeps from Chad's game slowly came to a halt. I felt my companions' eyes turning to me, burning into my skin.

"Wh-what did you figure out, Alan?" Garrett asked hesitantly.

I turned to face him. "How do people remember their lives? Not by the exact days, but by their experiences. How many of us remember the exact hour before this one? Or even the exact day before yesterday?"

"What do you mean?" Joy asked. "We *do* remember hours and days. I could tell you everything I did yesterday."

"Yeah," Belinda agreed. "How can you not remember what happened to you an hour ago?"

I pressed my palms together, trying to find the right words to explain what I was thinking. "Do you remember what time it was when you were first injured?"

The red-headed girl pursed her lips, considering this question.

"No, I don't."

"Exactly," I said. "But even without knowing the exact hour it happened, you probably remember *how* you were injured, *who* injured you, and how you felt. Try and think about it. What comes to mind?"

Belinda was silent for a moment, recalling the memory. "I was, maybe, four years old when I first skinned my knees." Her crystal-blue eyes gazed reminiscently downward. "I was chasing a big fish I saw outside the enclosure, when I tripped in the beet garden and fell on my knees. They hurt a lot at the time, so I cried."

She smiled sadly and added, "It was a really pretty fish, and I was devastated when it swam away."

Turning back to the others, I said, "If I can create my own version of time, I think I can actually make this time machine."

"And this version of time would be based off your own memory?" Chad asked, one finger perched ponderously under his chin.

I nodded emphatically, excited that my half-baked idea actually made some sort of sense.

"But there's a problem with that," Chad then added. "The only life that you've lived is your own. Our goal is to prevent the destruction of the colonies in the stars, which happened *hundreds* of years before you were born."

My smile drooped a little. I hadn't considered that.

"There's a recording of the Mars colony's destruction in the database," Garrett said. He shot me an encouraging glance. "If Alan can watch that, I'm sure he can imagine what it was like to be there when everything fell apart. It won't be *his* memory, but it will be a memory of the event."

"I was just going to suggest that!" Sal said, an optimistic smile stretching across his face. "Let's try it!"

Without another word, he hurried past me toward the screen, tapping his fingers on several glowing icons. The projections of my notes, Belinda's artwork, and Chad's game disappeared as Sal tapped on several new icons—these glowing deep red—that flashed across the screen. Each was named with a series of numbers and letters, and Sal slid his hands over them until he found an icon entitled *STANLEY*. He tapped to open it.

Suddenly, the screen darkened to an ominous pitch-black. We watched uneasily as a rainbow of lights fizzled into view, twirling and twisting frenziedly until they stabilized into one single hologram displaying something that existed only in a Terra-Maran's fantasy—a field of emerald-green grass.

My eyes grew wide with wonder.

"It's so beautiful..." Chad exhaled in a distant, awe-struck voice.

From the top of the hologram, a baby slowly crawled into view. It was only months old, with bare porcelain feet poking out of Terra-Mar's historic blue and orange robe. It grinned up at us, a tuft of dark hair upon its chubby head and a sparkle in its caramel eyes.

"Aw," Belinda sighed, tilting her head in adoration.

"How cute!" Joy chuckled.

The image shook slightly as the operator of the camera moved closer. A hand with matching complexion to the baby's came into view, its fingers long and slender like a woman's. She tapped the child lightly on the nose and the baby giggled, revealing a plush patch of toothless pink gums. My friends and I all softened, reveling in the memory of childhood.

"Stanley, my little Stanley," the woman behind the recorder cooed. "Can you say, 'Mommy'? Can you say that? Hm?"

"Mah!" Stanley squealed, and reached one tiny hand up to cling onto his mother's finger.

The woman chuckled. "Well, maybe in a few more months."

"Hey, Tasha," a man's voice said from behind the camera. "You want to go to the restaurant now? It's getting close to lunchtime."

The image shifted again as the camera tilted up toward the person who spoke. He had a long, angular face that was slightly scruffy around the chin and his lips curled upward in a loving smile.

The man approached across the sprawling green expanse, the bottom of his robe rippling as he walked. His hair was black, like the baby's, and shined beneath what was possibly the sun.

They must be in a park, I thought fascinatedly. *One of those outside places where people went to spend their leisure time.*

Some distance behind the man, a group of teenagers called to each other, throwing a red discus back and forth. Between them bounded a furry creature with long, gray hair—a *dog,* from what I'd read in our zoological texts. It barked enthusiastically whenever the discus passed over it.

And in the background, stretching far into the horizon, was what appeared to be a colossal forest of towering crystals, their jagged tips reaching majestically into the endless blue sky. They glistened in various enchanting colors—pale aquamarine, bright honey, luscious fern—casting rainbow-colored prisms all around themselves. The inhabitants moved peacefully around them, carrying curious holographic devices. Some spilled out in waves of ocean-blue and flaming orange, streaming to and fro over the gravel-lined terrain, which sparkled like the quartz of Terra-Mar's old classroom.

This is a metro on Mars, I realized, my heart leaping with excitement.

I'd always imagined what they had looked like, but I was finally seeing it with my own eyes.

But out of all the extraterrestrial wonders, the only part I could focus on was the sky.

A blue sky, I thought enviously at the hologram. Of course the sky on Mars wasn't truly blue, that metro had been engineered to resemble the real skies on the surface of Earth. *I'd expect nothing less from the ingenious ancestors of Terra-Mar.*

Reaching little Stanley, the man who must have been his father knelt down to collect him, bouncing him gently in his arms as he stood. Stanley laughed, and everyone in the lab laughed, too, filling our lonely room with an otherworldly delight.

"It's a little early, don't you think?" Tasha asked, off screen. "Our reservation isn't until one thirty."

"I'm sure they can squeeze us in for an early seating," the man said with a shrug and grin. Behind him came a burst of cheers as one of the youths caught the discus and thrust it back into the air, invoking another round of barks from the dog. It bounded after the object, its bright pink tongue flopping out of the side of its mouth.

A low roar suddenly interrupted the tranquil scene. With a start, the teenagers looked in the direction of the crystal forest, letting their disc to crash to the ground, forgotten. Even the dog halted and followed their gazes, a cautious growl rising up from its throat. In the distance, the stream of people between the towering gems slowed, turning to each other in confusion.

"What was that?" the father asked, turning his back to the camera. In his arms, Stanley moaned in discomfort.

Then came the screams, low and eerie at first, trickling in through the speakers and filling the lab with a disturbing screech.

The image shuddered as Tasha trotted to the man, pointing her camera over his shoulder. "What's going on over there?"

Then, one of the farthest buildings began to crumble, the structure fragmenting into shards as it crumbled to the ground. A second roar—this one much closer—soon followed, and the building across from the first crumbled as well.

"Something's destroying them," Garrett whispered, his words faint and apprehensive.

Soon, the waves of blue and orange began to ripple as the people near the falling buildings ran for the park, their arms wrapped around their heads, their gaping mouths howling for help.

Stanley's father whipped back around, his previously serene expression now replaced by alarm. "It's the Earth Purists! They've finally revolted! Run!"

Earth Purists? I thought quizzically. *Who were they? And why would they revolt in a beautiful place like that?*

A blur of green, blue, and brown flashed across the hologram as Tasha turned quickly to run in the opposite direction, the camera swinging violently in her hand with every hurried step. Her breath billowed out of the speakers in raspy pants, filling the sprawling lab with the mayhem of her world.

"Who would do this?" Joy asked in outrage.

We were all wondering the same thing.

My breaths, slow and steady just a moment ago, now quickened with Tasha's. At this point, I could imagine everything that she was feeling—the pounding of her feet against the lawn, the rush of air against her skin as she ran. Her confusion. Her fear.

Good, I thought, training my eyes unwaveringly on the hologram. *This is exactly what I need to see to create the time machine.*

Eventually the camera bounced out of Tasha's hands, sending a loud *boom,* followed by a series of clatters through the lab. A collective shiver spread throughout us as we watched snippets of the Martian metro spin on the hologram—the grass, the crumbling buildings, the screaming people fleeing for their lives. I clutched my stomach as a brief bout of dizziness overcame me, making me feel like I was actually there, tumbling through the park as well. When the camera finally landed and the spinning stopped, the only thing we saw was the top half of a woman lying on the ground, her black hair tangled over her scalp in a mixture of blood and sweat.

Stanley's mother was gone.

And we never even got to see her face.

Belinda gasped and Joy covered her eyes. Sal stammered a shocked, "Wh-what?"

All I could do was cup my hand over my mouth and resist the urge to vomit. My mind reeled with anger, sadness, and confusion. *Who were these terrible Earth Purists? Were Stanley and his father still alive?*

In the background, a glistening cloud grew as the remaining buildings crumbled one by one. The people beneath them continued to scream for their lives and rush forward in hordes—where they were headed, I wasn't sure. The teens who had been playing with the discus swept past the recorder while the dog snarled futilely at the oncoming obliteration that roared through the speakers like some otherworldly monster.

My fingertips and toes numbed with cold as I reconsidered my conviction to experience my ancestors' ruin. What I was seeing was just so hideous and despicable.

So this was what really happened on Mars.

This was what destruction looked like.

Hesitantly, I stepped away from the control panel. Imagining all this was one matter, but actually seeing it was different. Seeing it made it real—so real that I didn't think I could handle it. I wasn't sure if I wanted to.

In fact, no, I didn't want to. I didn't want to make the fear, pandemonium, and suffering of these people real. I was foolish to think that this would be easy. Please, no more, no more...

But then I remembered the reason for it all.

I could save these people. I could go back in time and stop this from ever happening. I just needed to see it first.

Sometimes you have to see something to truly understand it.

And so I did. I forced my eyes to stay open, enduring the torture as the towers continued to crumble and the people continuing to run, their bodies merging together into one big shoving mass. Some of them stumbled and fell, only to be trampled to death by those behind them. The glittering clouds rolled ominously closer, the last of the towers eventually erased from the planet's surface, leaving the once proud metro a barren wasteland of the cosmos.

Don't close your eyes, Alan. Keep watching.

And then, a sign of hope. A small fleet of space crafts emerged from the ruin many miles away, hovering over the destruction as if the operators were deciding whether or not to save the Martian people.

Our fall from the stars, I thought morbidly, feeling my knees weaken as I gazed up at the gleaming vehicles. Their pointed ends ignited with blazing-hot fire as they streaked out into the endless clutches of space. I could practically feel the wind from the combustions, the shards stinging against my skin, the agony of the dying people around me.

But no amount of hope could stop the sudden swell of the grass as the next explosion erupted beneath the ground, swallowing the image in a spray of dirt. We were blind, only able to listen to the mysterious sounds howling through the speakers—screeching human voices, the rocketing cries of the flaming space crafts, and the continuous *boom* of further detonations. The sounds vibrated through me, shaking me to the core. For a moment, I felt like I too was being pulled apart by whatever abominable means the Earth Purists used to destroy the humble Martian metro.

And then, silence.

It was finally over.

Tasha, Stanley, Stanley's father—they were all gone.

Everyone was gone.

And it was all real. It happened hundreds of years ago, but we were experiencing their deaths all over again.

They were all real.

When some feeling returned to my body, I found myself kneeling on the floor, tears flooding down my cold cheeks. I tried to speak and a helpless whimper crawled out of my throat. Somewhere in the back of my mind, I recalled that my companions were in the lab with me, but that's not how I felt. All I felt now was alone, in the vast, endless vacuum of outer space.

Now I knew how it felt to be on that planet, screaming and running for my life as everything I'd ever known exploded into clouds of dust and smoke. Now I knew what it felt like to lose everything that was ever familiar to me—everything I ever cared for or loved.

And I wished I didn't. I wished that I didn't know.

I wished that none of us did.

"That was our fall from the stars," Ruben said behind me, lower and more tragic than usual.

Weakly, I pressed my palms to the floor, shivering when the cold of the tiles sucked away what little remaining heat was in my skin. I turned around to see my teacher standing behind my friends. The noise from the recording had been so loud that it had drowned out the familiar hum of the elevator when Ruben entered the lab.

"Now you've seen it. Now you know. Now you've lived and died with them."

My friends continued to stare at the long-vanished hologram, as if the recording were still playing. The color from Belinda's usually pink cheeks had drained, leaving her looking as pale as a ghost, while Joy's hands still covered her face, tears seeping through her fingers. Sal's expression was stony and serious, and Chad and Garrett stood stiffly, their chests rising and falling with labored breaths.

Slowly, I pushed myself up to my feet, wobbling slightly. With one slow look around the lab—the pristine white walls and sleek gleaming tiles—I reminded myself that I was still alive.

Looking straight at Ruben, I said in a quivering tone, "I know how to create the time machine now."

CHAPTER 7

The seven of us marveled at the once-mythical contraption standing before us.

The time machine was a three-ton capsule that measured six feet tall and three and half feet wide. It had a thick steel exterior, a film-like mid-layer, and a translucent plastic interior. At its front was a simple metal door.

On the floor around us were the unused sheets and wires that we'd spent so much time fastening and coating, a symbol of our previously wasted efforts to build the time machine by hand.

"Do you think it'll work?" Joy asked nervously.

"I know it will," I answered. I hadn't watched the recording of people dying in the city of gems for nothing.

"We should test it before we go all the way back in time," Chad suggested. "Just to make sure."

"Great idea, Chad," Belinda said. Then, to me she added, "Alan, it's only fitting that you take the first trip. Is there a moment in your recent past that you think would be safe for you to return to?"

I tilted my gaze downward, sifting through my memories of the last couple of days.

"Yeah, I've got one."

Lifting my chin, I looked at each person in turn—Belinda and her ravishing red hair, fair and righteous Chad, conscientious Joy, strong-willed Sal, and of course, Garrett, the timid yet level-headed boy with whom I felt the greatest connection.

Finally, I focused on Ruben, who stood behind them all with his trusty tablet in hand, ready to take notes on this special occasion.

All of a sudden, I felt like I was about to lose them all. I was sure that the time machine would work, but only now did I realize the consequences of my success. I had created this contraption to travel back in time, and every action I took once I went back would inevitably change the course of the future. Once I stepped into it, it was very possible that I would never come back to this moment again. Was I about to lose my friends forever?

"Wherever your destination may lie," my teacher said, his eyes fixing solemnly on me from behind the glasses I created for him. "I'm sure that everything will be well."

Everything will be well.

I forced a small grin, and with a heavy heart, turned back to the machine. Stepping forward, I hooked my finger into a small hole at the corner of the door and pulled it open, revealing the shady cavity within. When I stepped onto the steel plate beneath, my weight triggered a string of fluorescent lights to glow to life, as I'd imagined they would.

In a moment of hesitation, I peered back over my shoulder, scanning the faces behind me. When I found Garrett's eyes, I held them, memorizing his hopeful expression.

It was the last thing I saw before I pulled the door closed.

Everything will be fine.

Alone in the capsule, I inhaled a deep breath and focused on the memory I chose for the test. The glowing lights distracted me, so I closed my eyes and tried to ignore the claustrophobia that was creeping up on me. I shifted my feet, my shoulders knocking against the capsule walls.

For a while, nothing happened, and I wondered if I had made a faulty machine after all.

Concentrate, Alan, I urged myself, balling my hands into frustrated fists.

Suddenly, the game of catch I'd played with Garrett four years ago returned to my mind, wiping away my other thoughts. I could smell the fragrance of the limes around us, feel the rough leather of the mitt against my hand, and see the look in the boy's eyes. For a few minutes of his life, he hadn't been a clumsy boy, but a daring rebel who'd snuck out of his pod to play with his friend.

At that moment inside the time machine, I felt happy and hopeful—the first time since the game of catch was a reality.

A low whir started in my ears, and I snapped my eyes open to see the capsule walls spinning around me, speeding faster and faster with each passing second. The whirring sound grew louder too, increasing with each revolution until it was almost deafening.

It was working. My time machine was actually working!

Weightlessness overcame me as my arms and legs floated up toward the ceiling. If the walls of the capsule weren't holding me in, I might've floated away forever.

Then, with panic, I realized that I'd been thinking of the wrong memory. "Wait! No, stop!" I shouted up at the machine. "Not *that* time!"

But it was too late. The walls spun faster and faster until the lights fused into a blazing wheel around me, and my stomach lurched with nausea.

I shoved against the capsule door, which had remained strangely stationery, and forced it open to find the lab replaced with a cold, infinite blackness, like the endless ocean.

I tumbled out into the void, unable to stop my momentum.

"Ruben?!" I cried, my voice echoing desolately. "Garrett?!"

And then, in a blinding flash of light, I was gone—torn painlessly into millions of cells that drifted aimlessly into the universe.

....

The next thing I knew, I was back in the lab, my friends all gathered around me. Littering the floor were the sheets of metal and wires that they were trying to piece together into some sort of functioning machine. Behind them, at the center of the lab, the elevator lay inactive on its platform.

For a second, I blinked confusedly, wondering where and *when* I had ordered the time machine to take me. But then, slowly and surely, I realized what was happening.

I was only back one day, right before I saw...

"I was just going to suggest that!" Sal said, an optimistic smile stretching across his face. "Let's try it."

He hurried past me toward the screen, tapping on several glowing icons until he found the one entitled *STANLEY.*

"No, don't open that!" I cried, leaping forward. I grabbed him by the shoulders and flung him roughly away from the panel, where he stumbled into Joy and Garrett.

"What was that about, Alan?" he bellowed once he'd regained his bearings. "I was just accessing the database for you!"

"That recording," I began, pointing a quivering finger at the control panel. Belinda and Chad stepped cautiously toward me. "It's awful! The destruction—Tasha, Stanley, Stanley's father! It's worse than your worst nightmare. Please, promise me you'll never *ever* watch it!"

I couldn't let them witness it again.

I couldn't let them see the destruction.

Joy crossed her arms and huffed. "What's gotten into you, Alan? You're talking nonsense."

"Do you already know what's in that file?" Chad asked suspiciously.

Garrett's eyes widened, waiting for my answer.

"Yes, I've seen the recording, and it's not good!" I cried hysterically. "I saw it right before I created the time machine. I'm from the future, and I know exactly what's going to happen after we open that file. That recording, it's really, *really bad.* Please, promise me you won't watch it. *Promise me!*"

Everyone gaped in disbelief. And it made sense for them to, because at that point we had still been eons away from understanding how to create the time machine. I wouldn't have believed that in just one day I could figure out what we'd been researching for four whole years, so why should they?

Inhaling deeply, I said, "In a few seconds, Ruben is going to come down the elevator to check our progress." To emphasize my point, I gestured to the platform, which was now ascending up to collect our teacher at the ground level.

Finally, my friends understood. Ruben's schedule had always been so erratic—no one could have predicted when he would visit. I had to have known. Their eyes shone with the bright glimmer of belief.

When the platform settled, they bounded excitedly through the mess of neglected materials to Ruben. His expression broke into surprise to see them approaching with such energy. He hadn't seen us excited about anything in four years.

"Ruben, it's done, the time machine is built!" Belinda announced. They others nodded emphatically, wide smiles stretching across their faces.

"Really?" he stammered, looking around. "Where is it?"

"I haven't created it yet," I said quietly from behind the group, still calming down from the incident with the video. "But tomorrow, I will. I'm here now as a test it to see if it works, and, well..." I lifted my arms and grinned. "It works."

"You, Alan—you came from the future?" Ruben asked again, awestruck.

I nodded and held out my palms up at him. "From tomorrow, more specifically." I scoffed internally at the ridiculousness of such a statement, but held Ruben's gaze so he'd know I was serious.

My teacher said nothing for a few seconds, just staring at me with unblinking eyes. Then he stepped backward, wobbling slightly, and clutched his dark curly head with shaking fingers. Slowly, a chuckle bubbled out of his throat, which morphed into a robust laugh. Soon he was in the throes of hysteria, joyful tears brimming from the edges of his eyes.

"You did it, Alan!" he guffawed, thrusting his arms into the air. "You've finally created the time machine!"

My friends cheered along with him, and embraced me in a big group hug. After four tedious years of sifting through endless data and reading the most obscure of topics, we'd finally done it

All of us, together, had finally created the time machine.

Ruben looked proudly upon his me and said, "So since you've already created the time machine in the future, can you do it again now? Can you do it right in front of our eyes?"

I smiled eagerly and pulled away from my friends to face the control panel. With palms outstretched, I closed my eyes and concentrated on my latest creation. I visualized the gleaming steel in my mind, felt its smoothness against my skin, and envisioned the glowing lights within.

Like always, the warming sensation surged down my spine and through my body, all the way to my fingertips. When I opened my eyes, the very same capsule that I would enter tomorrow stood in front of me again.

I could feel the whole group exhale together as they marveled at this fascinating vehicle, gravitating toward it with *oohs* and *ahhs*.

Ruben adjusted his glasses ponderously and said in a low voice, "Humanity has always dreamed of mastering time, only to fail each time they tried. But you did it, Alan. You did it."

I tried to smile at my teacher's praise, but all I could think about was the video of the Mars colony's destruction. Before I'd traveled back in time, my friends had experienced the deaths of the early Terra-Marans with me, however awful that experience had been. But now that I'd spared them of that horrible recording, I felt somehow...

Lonely.

Had Ruben seen the recording before that moment? I wasn't sure, but the possibility that he hadn't was harrowing. If he hadn't, that would mean I was the only person to have witnessed the destruction of my ancestors. I was the only one who knew how important their demise was to the creation of the time machine.

I carried that weight alone now.

Pushing the thought aside, I turned to Ruben. "So I guess I'm going back in time now, huh?"

"Yes of course," my teacher said wistfully. "That's been our goal for the past four years." He perched one hand beneath his chin. "I must know, Alan—what facilitated the breakthrough? How did you suddenly figure it out?"

I hesitated. "Um, it was a recording that we found in the database."

I paused, waiting for Ruben to say something like, *Oh, I see,* or, *Very good, Alan,* but he just looked at me, waiting for the rest of the explanation. I continued, "It showed the destruction of a metro on Mars. When I watched it, I—" I paused again, searching for the right words. Finally I settled on the same ones Ruben had used from that alternate reality. "I lived and died with them."

Still Ruben said nothing, just watching my friends circle the time machine.

Inhaling a deep breath, I said wearily, "Well, it's time for me to save humanity, I guess."

"Actually," Ruben answered, holding his hands up haltingly, "I think we should wait."

I looked at him in bafflement. "Why?"

My teacher lowered his arms and crossed them together in front of him, regaining his familiar lecturing stance. "You've achieved your greatest feat yet by creating this time machine. Let's dig for some more data, and see what else your abilities can do?"

I stared, speechless. After pushing me and my friends for so many years to create the time machine, now Ruben was telling me not to take the last step and save the Mars colony?

"But—" I started.

"Just think of the possibilities," he interrupted, his eyes blazing with that ambitious flame again. "If you were successful enough to bend all of time and space to your will, there's no telling what else you could do—what else you could *create.* Entire planets, stars, galaxies—you could control universes, Alan!"

With a suspenseful pause, Ruben gazed at me, wild with fanaticism. "You could create *living things*—human beings! You are the Creator, after all. You can bring anything into existence, as long as you imagine it so."

I couldn't believe what I was hearing.

Ruben had always been so careful with what he taught me to create. They were always just things—structures to help support the metro, mostly.

But now he was telling me to create living, thinking beings.

He was telling me to be *God.*

Before either of us could say anything, a sickening *crunch* drew our attention toward the time machine. To our astonishment, we turned to see it lying, bent, on the floor. Its crumpled door was jerked open and the glowing lights inside flickered until they went dark.

"What..." I began breathlessly, but the words caught in my mouth. I'd weighed the bottom of the capsule with three tons of metal. Nothing less than a bulldozer could have tipped it so easily.

Around the fallen machine stood my equally astonished friends—all except Garrett, who stumbled out from behind it with a shocked expression and trembling hands. Stopping a few feet away from the other children, the timid boy reluctantly looked in my direction, his forest-green eyes wide with guilt.

The evidence was undeniable.

Garrett had broken the time machine.

"*You!*" Ruben spat.

Realizing the trouble he'd made for himself, Garrett cringed and cowered as the teacher stomped over to him, finger pointed accusingly.

"*You!* It's always been *you!*"

"I don't know how it happened, I swear!" Garrett cried, distraught.

Ruben roared. "The ruined blocks, the crumpled sheet metal, *the dent beneath the enclosure!* It was all *you!*"

How does he know about the dent? I wondered, stunned. It was barely noticeable, and had happened years ago...

"You've been nothing but trouble since the moment you were born!" my teacher bellowed. My friends and I watched with horror as Garrett sank to the cold stone floor.

"Ruben, please," I said weakly, holding out a hand. "I can just create a new time machine. It's not that big of a deal."

But Ruben either didn't hear or didn't care, because he kept on berating the poor boy.

"You ruin everything you touch. A practical Earth Purist!"

"Stop it!" Sal demanded.

"It's not his fault," Joy pleaded.

My teacher puffed his chest, towering over Garrett. With a terrifying snarl, he leaned down until he was eye to eye with the boy and hissed, "You *Scatter!*"

The lab fell silent.

That was too far. All the Scatters we'd heard about from childhood stories were rough and heartless—brutes that plundered through everything around them. They caused the type of destruction that I saw in the hologram of what happened on Mars. That was not Garrett at all. He was the gentlest person I knew.

Curling his legs up against his chest, Garrett whimpered, "No, no, I'm not a Scatter! I'm a Builder, like the other Terra-Marans. I'm not a Scatter! I'm not!"

"I knew you were a Scatter all along!" Ruben said, his lips peeling back over his teeth in disgust. "I saw all the signs. I should've alerted the rest of the metro sooner!"

"No, I'm not a Scatter! *I'm not!*" Garrett continued futilely.

I shook my head. Why was Ruben being so cruel? He knew it would take me less than a minute to create a new time machine—this wasn't about that. This was a personal attack.

Garrett was the one who'd always encouraged me to believe in the good I was doing for Terra-Mar, even when I didn't believe in it myself. He'd gotten us all to start working together again when were at each other's throats over our futile research. His contribution to our group was palpable—he was the glue that held us together.

Why was Ruben acting like Garrett's life didn't matter?

Then, without warning, the cowering boy looked up at the teacher with an eerie expression, something vaguely like...

Rage.

At the sight of him, Ruben took an involuntary step back, his eyes widening in what could only be described as fear. Garrett crouched like an animal about to attack.

But Ruben quickly came to, and with an unexpectedly powerful sweep of his arm, the teacher grabbed the boy by his sweater collar and dragged him, stumbling, toward the elevator. Garrett's shoes slapped against the tile floor of the lab as he struggled—*clap, clap, clap.*

"No! Stop! Please! I don't want to go to the Scatter settlement!" Garrett shrieked, desperately trying to pry Ruben's hands off.

"There's no place for you here, *Scatter!*" Ruben shouted viciously, refusing to release the struggling boy. "You're no good to the Builders of Terra-Mar!"

"I'm not a Scatter!" Garrett hollered, thrashing in agony. "Stop calling me that! I'm not a Scatter! I'm not!"

Suddenly Sal leapt at the teacher, grabbing him with two slender arms.

"Don't do it, Sal!" Belinda shouted.

"Let him go!" Joy screamed, jumping up to help Sal.

With a backhanded slap, Ruben knocked them off and twisted around to grab them too, gripping them by the necks of their sweaters with his free hand. "Don't think I don't know what you two have been up to, also! Sal, you've been starting fights with the other children in your locale every morning, and Joy, I've seen you having fits with the children outside the classrooms when you go back to your pod every night. Neither of you are any better than this one here. You're all Scatters!"

Ruben hauled them all toward the tiny elevator while Belinda, Chad, and I gaped in shock. I wanted to do something, but I felt paralyzed.

It was all because of me.

If I hadn't come back in the time machine, none of this would have happened.

Ruben stopped in front of the tiny platform, his hands clutched unyieldingly on the three struggling teens, and stared up through the tiny shaft. The four of them would never fit all at once.

He turned his fury in my direction. "Alan, create a bigger elevator!"

"But—" I began.

"CREATE A BIGGER ELEVATOR, NOW!"

Frantically, I thrust my palms out at the far end of the lab, feeling a hot burn through my body. Within seconds, a large steel box appeared beside my teacher, the entire structure enclosed within a shaft stretching up to the ground level.

Ruben dashed into the new elevator, the three children screeching with terror, and flew up toward the metro in a frenzied gust of air, leaving behind only the vacant shaft.

Without thinking, I dashed toward the old platform and leapt onto it just as it began ascending.

"What are you doing, Alan?" Belinda yelled from behind me.

"They're Scatters, don't go after them!" Chad called.

"They're *not* Scatters!" I cried vehemently, dropping to one knee and pressing my palms against the metal. "They're our *friends!*"

A storm of sparks danced from my fingertips, and before I could prepare myself, the platform careened up the elevator shaft at an impossible speed, pushing me flat from the force. My head knocked against the metal with a *thunk*, but I grit my teeth against the pain. With my arms pressed to the steel at my sides, I clenched my eyes shut, feeling the merciless onrush of air.

When the elevator hit the ground level, I was launched into the air, my arms wheeling weightlessly by my sides. I dropped back down on top of a nearby coconut tree, falling through its flapping leaves and sliding down its trunk, the spiky bark scraping ripping open my sweater before I landed face-first on the ground.

The skin on my back was raw and I suspected I might have broken something, but I pushed myself onto my knees regardless of the pain. When the dizziness faded, I found the steel box standing empty in the middle of the clearing where my friends and I had stacked blocks all those years ago. A group of gardeners, their dirt-stained spades held loosely in their hands, gathered curiously around it, wondering where it lead to.

"Scatters!" Ruben's voice echoed from above. "There are Scatters among us! Call the Neptuans immediately! We must be on high alert!"

I caught sight of the teacher already atop the staircase on the lowest level of Zeta, his three captives still grappling unsuccessfully with him. Nearby, the Terra-Marans spilled out of their pods to stare in his direction.

"Scatters?" they murmured questioningly to each other.

"They still exist?"

"Well, we certainly can't keep them here!"

"We need to send them away!"

"Call the Neptuans!" Ruben repeated hysterically. He called to the radio operators stationed at the far end of the ground level, behind the trees and shrubbery near me. "We need to send these fiends to the Scatter settlement!"

The operators nodded emphatically and ripped the mouthpiece from the radio's side, pressing a series of buttons until it crackled to life. By now, Ruben had already waded through the crowds forming around him and climbed halfway up to the mid level.

"No, we don't!" I hollered at them, wobbling to my feet. "They're not Scatters! They're just Builders!"

But my words were drowned out by the Terra-Marans' panicked voices. The idea of Scatters existing in the community was too terrifying for them to see reason.

I rushed toward the stairs leading to Zeta and climbed as fast as I could. My balance wavered from the fall and I teetered right and left, feeling like my jostled brain was about to slip out of my skull.

The teacher and his detainees proceeded relentlessly past the mob that had formed at the mid level and went on to the top level. Outside the enclosure, a large crystalline structure drifted into view, its jagged exterior glittering from the fluorescent lights like a bejeweled ghost. It sailed gracefully through the water until it reached the docking pod at the top level, where it moored in the nest of curled metal beams outside.

The Neptuan Transporters! I thought in panic. I tried to quicken my pace as I reached the platform of the lowest level, but the crowd had thickened. *They must've already been in the area when the operators called them.* Maneuvering through the furiously packed bodies, I frantically climbed up the next set of stairs.

"Send them away! Send them away!" the Terra-Marans chanted, their fists raised high in rage.

The muffled grinding of gears reverberated through the glass as a translucent bridge extended from the Neptuan vessel, attaching to the hatch with a loud *clunk*. When it had drained of sea water, I could see dark fragmented figures marching toward the pod.

Faster, Alan! I thought urgently, sweat pouring down my forehead.

"Send them away! Send them away!"

Pushing through the frenzied hordes, I watched in dread as Ruben and the three adolescents arrived at the top level, only a sprint away from the docking pod's entrance. So close to exile now, my friends had transitioned from struggling to full-on hysteria, screaming fruitlessly for help.

"Ruben!" a man called, stepping out from the gathering behind the teacher. He was tall, with short black hair and olive skin. He motioned toward Garrett. "What are you doing with my son?"

"Your son is a Scatter!" Ruben spat back at him, his brow glistening with sweat. "Look upon the face of your own flesh and blood—no longer will he sully your clean hands. He's going to the settlement!"

"Send them away! Send them away!"

The man looked hard at Garrett, whose cheeks were stained with salty tears. Shaking his head in disappointment, the man turned and disappeared into the mass of scowling faces and waving fists.

I can't believe it, I thought incredulously, panting as I neared the top level, my legs aching from the long climb. *Garrett's own father didn't even stand up for him—all because Ruben called him a Scatter.*

Why didn't anyone question Ruben? They *knew* Garrett. They knew he wasn't a Scatter.

Didn't they?

Turning back to the bridge, the teacher reached for the handle and flung it vehemently open just as the Transporters entered through the hatch opposite him. They wore some sort of opaque black material and held shock batons—rods sizzling with electricity at their ends.

With a great heave, Ruben hurled the three teens inside at the exact moment I reached the top level.

Shoving my way through the crowd, I dashed for the door, but I wasn't fast enough. Ruben slammed it, locking, in my face with a violent *BANG.*

I bashed my fists against the glass window, shouting at the Transporters encircling the frightened trio. "No! Don't take them! They're not Scatters! Leave them alone!"

Soon there were hands at my shoulders, pulling me away from the bridge. I flailed and screamed for my release.

Inside the pod, there was a flurry of motion as the Transporters raised the shock batons over the three children, who clung together and stared up at the belligerent strangers in horror.

"No! Stop!" I shouted at the closed door.

"There's nothing you can do for them now, Alan," Ruben said gravely, tightening his grip on me. "They're Scatters, and there's nothing in the world that can change that."

"Send them away! Send them away!"

The first strike went to Sal, who raised his hands above his head as a burst of sparks encompassed his body. He fell limply to the floor a moment later.

"No!" I yelled, my vision blurring with tears.

"Send them away! Send them away!"

I could see Joy's lips mouthing *You know me! You know who I am!* to her former fellow Neptuans, but they beat her anyway, knocking her to the ground next to Sal. Her braided hair had become an unruly mess of golden strands.

"Please stop hurting them!" I cried helplessly, my voice cracking.

"Send them away! Send them away!"

Finally they turned to Garrett, the shock baton descending so quickly upon him that he barely had time to defend himself. His body dropped weakly.

I watched speechlessly as the Transporters grabbed the three children off the floor. When they dragged Garrett to his feet, he was trembling all over. He peered despondently back over his shoulder, a wide red patch over his left temple where they'd struck him. His eyes drooped half-open with near unconsciousness.

This was every child's worst nightmare—to be exiled to the Scatter settlement.

"I'm so sorry..." I wept, my muscles going limp at the sight of the timid boy now battered and bruised. "I'm sorry I couldn't protect you..."

"Send them away! *Send them away!*"

"You can't help them, Alan!" Ruben cried, shaking me. "They are what they are. *No one can help them!*"

And then, like a passing shadow, Garrett's expression changed. His brows narrowed odiously beside his swollen temple, and the sides of his lips curved downward in a contemptuous glare.

Blinking my tears away, I wondered if I'd hit my head so hard that I was seeing things. In a split-second, Garrett turned from a fearful little soul to something else... something that I didn't recognize. He looked...

Frightening.

But whatever rage lied under the surface, he didn't have a chance to act on it. With a heartless *CLANG*, the Transporters closed the hatch behind them, taking my friends from the metro for good.

CHAPTER 8

I knelt on the bridge, my arms hanging limply by my sides. I stared straight ahead into the vacant docking pod, half-expecting my friends to walk back through despite the fact that the glittering Neptuan submarine had long departed. In my mind I willed the hatch to swing open and return my friends to me, but unfortunately, I knew that wouldn't happen.

"None of this was your fault, Alan," Ruben said, resting one hand on my shoulder. "People are what they are, and they'll never change."

I couldn't speak. I couldn't even look at him. I refused to believe that my teacher—*our* teacher—had so blatantly betrayed three of his brightest students. They'd spent the last four years of their lives searching through data for him, only to be tossed to the Neptuan Transporters like meat to piranhas.

Sal, Joy, Garrett. They were all gone.

Lowering himself to one knee, Ruben peered at me through his sweat-stained glasses. The air was thick with superiority as the Terra-Marans congratulated each other for ridding themselves of the Scatters—the first ones they've seen in decades. Soon they would return to their normal routines, blissfully ignorant of the terror they'd just inflicted.

"Don't feel sorry for them, Alan," my teacher said softly. "The Scatters feed off of sympathy, but they'll never fulfill your hopes. They think that they can take from us forever and never give anything in return, but we've just proven that they can't. People like that have no place among the Builders of Terra-Mar. It's for the best that they're gone."

I kept my eyes focused furiously on the docking pod. If I looked at Ruben now, I might punch him in the face, and I didn't want to start any more commotion than what has already occurred. How could he so easily disregard three students who'd committed themselves to his research for such a large portion of their lives? Was there really such an obvious standard that defined Scatters? Or Builders? Or people in general? I'd always been told that Builders created with their hands, and Scatters did nothing but destroy what the Builders made.

And what about me? For as long as I'd lived, I had never built anything useful with my hands. All the comforts of Terra-Mar originated from my mind, not from my strain and sweat. Did that make me a Scatter, too? Did my lack of physical effort make me something to be despised?

What if, one day, Ruben accused *me* of being a Scatter? Would people blindly believe him like they did of my friends?

"I don't believe they're Scatters," I muttered stonily.

With a patronizing smile and a pat on my shoulder, my teacher said, "Well, they're not here anymore now, so it's time to move on to more important things."

He stood back up and trotted toward the stairs, his footsteps making soft *pangs* on the steel ground. When he got to the landing, he paused and turned back to me. "I understand that this day has been a bit... *emotional.* But I do expect you to be back in the lab as soon as possible for your next project."

My jaw dropped open. How could he expect me to do more research after watching three of my closest friends be beaten and marched away into the Scatter settlement?

"I meant what I said back in the lab," he continued. "I believe we should pursue your ability to create living things. Belinda and Chad can help you collect information about how living organisms work—consumption, respiration, reproduction, all the basic functions."

My eyes fell to the gaps in the grated platform, where young children and their parents milled between their pods.

Was this real, or just part of my imagination?

"I know all that may seem daunting at first," Ruben continued coolly. "But like your research for the time machine, it will all be much easier once you work from the end back to the beginning."

My head snapped up at his words, suddenly alert.

That was Garrett's idea—to start at the end and work back toward the beginning.

Would a Scatter have thought of that?

Without another word, Ruben descended the stairs, his footsteps disappearing into the buzz of the vast metro beneath. The metro that I created based on his teachings.

"I'll be expecting you no later than nine o' clock tomorrow morning," he called back. "Don't be late."

....

After a sleepless night, I found myself back in the lab, surrounded by the scraps of the broken time machine. It was lying on its side in front of the control panel, the dormant inside cavity exposed behind the hanging door. My mother had given me a new sweater which itched with starchy newness. Behind me, Ruben stood with Belinda and Chad, all of them waiting quietly.

With unfeeling fingers, I raised my palms to the machine and imagined it new, the usual sensation of my ability dulled by my reluctance. Within seconds, an identical time machine flickered into existence next to the broken one.

I dropped my arms to my sides, defeated.

Sighing in relief, Ruben rushed past me toward the new capsule.

"Wonderful as always, Alan," he said, his fingers running admiringly over the smooth steel exterior. "Wonderful as always."

Yes, that's right. My creations were wonderful, as Ruben had always thought they were. I was the Creator, after all. And that was what I did—create.

After one more circle around the time machine, my teacher promptly gravitated toward the control panel, bringing the screen to life with the touch of his hand.

"Now that everything is sorted out," he began briskly, sliding his hands across the sleek surface, "We can finally begin our next project: creating *life.*"

A rainbow of lights projected onto the hologram, twisting and twirling until they stabilized to a recording of one cell splitting into two.

Chad and Belinda approached from behind, glancing at me worriedly. When our eyes met, they quickly averted their gazes.

Were they ashamed to acknowledge me? Did they think doing so would get them sent to the Scatter settlement too?

"To make another life form is the epitome of creation," my teacher began, his eyes trained eagerly on the hologram. "Our new goal will be to help the Creator understand how a human being functions: how it eats, sleeps, make decisions, forms relationships with other human beings, and so on. Once he understands these, she can create the perfect race of humans—one in which Builders are the dominant demographic, and Scatters are completely eliminated from the gene pool."

He talks about a human being as if they were objects, I thought resentfully.

I looked to the fiery-haired girl and the reed-like boy standing stiffly behind Ruben, wondering if they also found our teacher's words insane.

Ruben paused as the two sister cells split apart on the hologram, forming a total of four now.

"But I thought Alan was going to go back in time and save the Mars colony?" Belinda asked in a small, hesitant voice. Chad nodded in agreement.

There was a heart-wrenching silence as Ruben turned slowly to face her, his fingers clenching into fists. Belinda drew back reflexively, waiting for him to strike, but after a moment he relaxed and smiled with pseudo-believability.

"Well, of course he will," Ruben said, "but after that happens, we might not ever see him again. Once he changes the course of humanity, he may never even discover his power to create, so before he's lost to us forever, we should collect as much information as we can about what he can do, don't you think?"

Belinda nodded stiffly as he went on, "Now that the Scatters have been removed from our midst, we can finally start *experimenting* with the Creator's ability—*challenging* him to see what other astounding things he can do."

The teacher peered over at me. "After all, an imaginative mind is a precious mystery. Who knows what extraordinary feats it can achieve."

Finally, Belinda and Chad met my eyes, both with utter fear and pity.

So this was my fate now—to become a glorified cog in the grand wheel that was the greatest teacher of Terra-Mar.

I was no longer Alan. I was just the Creator now. That person—that *thing* that brought life to the metro.

And from that point forth, everything became a routine. I arrived in the lab every morning at 09:00 and spent my days researching life – always under the close supervision of Ruben so that I would not become distracted by using the time machine. With Belinda and Chad at my side,

I watched videos of flowers blooming, tadpoles growing into frogs, even the mating rituals of animals, all in the attempt of trying to create them exactly as they appeared to me.

During this time, Scatter sightings became more frequent in Terra-Mar. Almost every week, a wailing child or teary-eyed adult would be dragged up to the docking pod to be beaten and swept away by the Neptuan Transporters. Soon, the metro's population decreased significantly, leaving a community full of scared, suspicious people.

After a year of unsuccessful research, Ruben grew impatient. He revealed the lab to the rest of the metro, and compelled many of the teachers to venture down and assist us. Because of his influence on me, he had the power to do anything he wanted in Terra-Mar, and everyone listened to him. And so, at his strict orders, I created Bunsen burners, beakers, test tubes, goggles, and measuring scales to accommodate the experiments that he planned to execute. Soon, the lab was no longer a haven for exploration, but a place full of anxious people marching to the beat of Ruben's drum for fear that they'd be labeled Scatters and sent away.

Belinda and Chad were extremely cooperative with Ruben's demands, directing our newest project members on the experiments of the day, every day. They never seemed to tire, or showed it if that's what they felt. They'd seen the consequences of disobedience, and wouldn't dare want to be sent away.

And I obeyed right along with them, but no longer with the enthusiasm I once had. I never even cared about going back in time to save the Mars colony – I only wanted to create the time machine so Ruben will continue calling me a good student. But more and more each day, I wondered if this was all there was to my life—to follow the ever-changing whimsies of a stubborn old man. Was there no higher purpose for myself, or for the Terra-Marans? I dared not ask out loud or risk being deemed a Scatter. After all, what good was I here if I didn't create?

On and on went the days, going down to the lab every morning, watching the new project members fuss over their experiments, tending to Ruben's questions, then ascend back up to the ground level only to discover that the Neptuan Transporters had just departed with another supposed Scatter. I retired to my pod each night, exhausted but unable to sleep, cursed to repeat the entire routine the next day.

Wake up, lab, Transporters, sleep.

What was I doing with my life?

Wake up, lab, Transporters, sleep.

Was this the kind of world I lived in?

Wake up, lab, Transporters, sleep.

Was this the kind of world I created?

On and on went the endless cycle. Every day, every week, every month, every year.

Until the morning it all disappeared—scattered into the endless ocean abyss.

PART 2

CHAPTER 9

I wake groggily on the mattress I created for myself just before falling asleep. The odor of my own sweat mixed with salty seawater wafts into my nose, and the steady hum of The Liberation's engine rings in my ears. A sharp pain streaks through my neck as I lift my head. I curse myself for not creating a pillow.

Pushing myself up to a sitting position, I find my wet shoes set neatly aside at the end of the mattress. The rest of the floor is still soaking too—the moisture seeps into my socks as I stand up. Running my hands sleepily through my hair, I look down at the baseball that I placed by the head of my bed. I hold it up to my eyes, turning it in my hands as if it had somehow changed during my brief hour or so of unconsciousness. But of course there's no change, so I stuff it into my pocket, satisfied. Trotting toward the control panel, I glance briefly up at the clock—where both hands point to 12—then gaze out of the front window at the endless ocean rushing past, the high beams casting ghostly rays into the darkness.

The lost Terra-Marans might all be out there, somewhere...

Or they might not, and I could just be wasting my time.

I reach up to the screen of trickling numbers and press the button beneath it, sending a few clicks of sonar out into the water. Expecting nothing to echo back, I entertain the thought of going back to sleep. But when I look up at the screen again, an unusual shape catches my attention.

"What *is* that?" I mutter, narrowing my eyes at the image.

Suddenly, footsteps coming pounding from behind—*pang, pang, pang*—making me jump. I turn to find five small faces poking out from the hole in the floor.

"Ha ha, we got out of the bedroom!" Shawn hollers, his mouth opened wide in an obnoxious laugh.

"You thought you could keep us locked down there, didn't you?" Lawrence cries victoriously.

Cal pushes his way through Shawn and Lawrence. "Well, you were wrong, and we got out!"

"The wheel isn't *that* hard to turn!" Beckett cackles.

Behind them all, Owen wobbles into view, trying to keep his footing on the ladder.

I press my hand over my leaping heart. "Don't scare me like that! Didn't I tell you to keep your voices—"

A sudden *clonk* sends me tumbling sideways toward the wall, where I slam against the icy window. The boys spill over too in a heap of flailing arms and legs. A deafening alarm begins to blare—*BONG! BONG! BONG!*

"Whoa!" Lawrence cries, popping up at the top of the heap. He covers his ears dramatically.

"Get off o' me, Lawrence!" Shawn complains from beneath the dough-faced boy.

"Ow, you poked my eye, Shawn!"

"What *was* that, guys?"

Behind them all, Owen rolls out into sight.

BONG! BONG! BONG!

Pressing my hands to my own ears, I turn to see the floor tilting up into an incline. The mattress begins sliding menacingly down toward me, my shoes bouncing heedlessly with it.

A second *clonk* tilts the ship in the opposite direction, and sends us all tumbling across the slippery floor. We slam against the opposite wall in a pile of limbs.

BONG! BONG! BONG!

"It's too loud!"

"Turn it off, Alan!"

"Would you all get off of me?" I scream back at all of them, elbowing someone's leg out of my face so I can push myself up off the window. "I don't even know what's going on."

A sharp movement in the ocean outside catches my eye, and I whip around to see it clearer. Looming up next to us is a giant crystalline structure almost the size of The Liberation. Its jagged exterior glitters in the light as it approaches.

"What *is* that?" Beckett screams over the alarm, squeezing next to me to look through the window.

I press my face against the glass again. "It's a Neptuan Transporter Sub! They must have been making their rounds when they saw us coming from Terra-Mar."

"Do you think they're here to help us find the lost Terra-Marans?" Owen yelps.

Before I can respond, the Neptuan submarine tilts its glittering bow toward The Liberation.

"W-what're they doing?!" Cal shouts.

My breath catches as I watch the ship shift into a menacing stance. "They don't recognize this vessel. They're attacking us! Everyone get back!"

A third *clonk*—this one rougher and more forceful—sends us careening wildly around the room. The boys, the mattress, my shoes, even the plastic bag of food all clatter and fly in the chaos.

"Make it stop! Make it stop!"

"I think I'm going to vomit!"

"No, don't vomit!" I scream. "No matter what you do, do not vom—"

Hitting a flat surface, I clench my eyes shut and hurriedly imagine a metal handle protruding from beneath my fingers. Grabbing quickly onto it, I open my eyes to find myself lying on the ceiling of the control room.

There's a tiny radio across from me, its unclipped mouthpiece clattering against the wall. Before The Liberation can make another rotation, I thrust myself forward, dodging Owen as he slides past me and ducking when the bag of provision shoots toward my head.

By the time I reach the radio, the submarine is already halfway turned in a new direction. I snatch the mouthpiece out of the air and slap my other hand against the wall nearby, creating another handle so I won't go flying.

"Neptua! Neptua!" I bark into the radio. "This is Alan, of Terra-Mar! Do you copy? I'm not a threat!"

Another impact sends me sailing across the room, slamming into Cal and Shawn. They shriek and wail as I grapple at thin air, trying to right myself.

BONG! BONG! BONG!

Gravity pulls me every which way as the ship tumbles. When one of my shoes spirals toward me, I duck out of the way and it hits Cal instead with a well-deserved, "Ow!"

Once again I see the radio across from me, and I fling myself toward the opposite wall, nearly tripping over the mattress in the process. Grabbing both the mouthpiece and the looped handle nearby, I holler into the radio again, "Neptua! Stop attacking us! We're from Terra-Mar! We need—"

Another *clonk* sends the submarine spinning again, but I hold stubbornly onto my handle.

"Neptua!" I scream, my legs dangling beneath me. "This is Alan, the Creator of Terra-Mar! Our metro has just been—"

"Did you just say you're the Creator?" a woman's voice crackles through the speaker.

My heart leaps.

"Yes, I'm the Creator! I'm on this vessel with five young children. Repeat: I'm on this vessel with five young children. We need a safe place to dock—"

The radio shrieks with static, then goes blank, leaving me to stare cluelessly at the mouthpiece.

BONG! BONG! BONG!

Soon, the rotations slow and the floor returns to my feet once again. I release the handle and scurry over to the control panel, where the crystalline structure glitters into the light of the high beams, traveling toward us head on.

In a panic, I grab a lever and push it all the way forward to aim the submarine's nose down toward the ocean floor—out of the way of the Neptuan's rapidly approaching ship. As everyone and everything in the cabin begins to shift again, I drop to my knees and hook my elbows around the control panel, locking myself onto it. The ocean floor materializes through the giant window in front of me and I thrust my hands forward, imagining the feeling of smooth metal. Within seconds, the top of a giant ramp appears in the high beams.

Hitting the ramp, The Liberation slides with a teeth-clenching *SHREEE*, the friction of the metal throwing sparks, even in the icy-cold water.

We skid off the end of the ramp, moving significantly slower now, and settle onto the ocean floor with a heavy *thump*. After a few minutes, the alarm finally ceases, leaving only the silence of the deep ocean around us.

I scan the control room, taking stock of the damage. At the far end, Lawrence and Shawn lie on top of each other, groaning. Owen dangles from the handle I created on the ceiling, his legs kicking futilely beneath him. At the left wall, Beckett and Cal stumble to their feet, then collapse dizzily back to the floor. Everyone appears completely traumatized, but no one seems seriously injured.

The radio crackles back to life, and I snatch the swinging mouthpiece from beneath it. "Neptua!" I call wearily. "This is the Creator speaking. Do you read me?"

We all hold our breath, waiting for a reply. But there is none. "Neptua!" I repeat. "This is the Creator! Can you confirm—"

Another familiar *clunk* comes from the hull, then the whirr of a draining bridge. I turn to the left window to see one of the Neptuan submarines settled next to us on the ocean floor.

Dropping the mouthpiece, I hurry to the hole in the floor—shoving the mattress from where it had landed on top of it—and climb down the ladder. I step with moist socks into the entry area, then face the hatch, the sound of heavy footsteps marching up from the bridge outside.

When the footsteps stop, I hold my breath, watching the wheel of the hatch creak slowly open. Before I can prepare myself, the hatch bursts open, knocking against the wall beside it with a jarring *clang*. A group of burly, stone-faced men in faded black clothes barge wordlessly inside, their boots thumping on the damp floor. Each of them holds a sleek black shock baton in his hand, the tip sizzling with electric sparks.

"Whoa, what's going on?" I sputter, holding out my hands and backing away. I'd never seen their weapons this close before.

A woman steps through them—or rather, a girl, with pale blue eyes and a sleek blonde ponytail. She can't be more than a few years older than me, but her gaze is as stern as the men around her, and she fixes it on me.

Before I can say anything, she raises her shock baton and strikes me with a burst of bright hot electricity. I cry out in agony as my body quivers and falls—*thud*—to the floor.

My mind flashes with the frightened faces of my old friends—Sal, Joy, Garrett—and I find myself back on the platform at Zeta, staring in horror as they're beaten by the same burly men who surround me now.

Is this how they felt when they were being taken away? I wonder fleetingly. *When they were being treated as dangerous, untrustworthy monsters instead of the scared children they really were?*

"Check the vessel," the girl orders in a deep, authoritative tone. "Make sure there are absolutely *no Scatters* onboard."

My eyes flicker open in time to see her point up the ladder.

The floor vibrates against my head as two of the men climb up to the control room. There, the boys shriek and howl, their small footsteps pounding, *pang, pang, pang.*

The girl gestures to the open hatch of the living quarters and orders, "Check in there, too. You never know where they're hiding."

The men jog heavily past me, splashing residual water in my face.

"W-why are you d-doing this?" I murmur as loudly as I can.

The girl looks down as if noticing me for the first time. "I apologize for this harsh greeting, Creator, but given the times, we have to make sure there are no Scatters aboard the vessel. You're obviously not one of them, but we've heard the rumors about your sympathies."

"Here are the children, Captain," one of the men in the control room announces through the hatch above us. He and his comrade present the boys' five distraught faces through the hole. "They're all under thirteen, so we can't tell which ones will be Scatters yet."

"Alan!" Owen calls. "Tell them not to hurt us!"

"All clear back there, Captain," another man reports, pointing to the living quarters. "We checked the engine room, too. No one."

"Good," the girl says firmly. Then, lowering herself to me, her expressions softens to a tight smile. "Creator, my name is Gina. I'm the captain of the Neptuan Transporters."

The shock fading slightly now, I push myself up to a sitting position. My clothes are soaked from lying on the floor, but I ignore the discomfort and weakly brush Gina's hand away.

"Not Creator, *Alan,* just Alan."

Gina's smile disappears and she rises to her feet, her gaze never leaving my face. The men eye me closely, their shock batons ready to strike at the first sign of retaliation.

"Alright, *Alan,*" she says. "Now that we've officially met, you can tell me why you're out here in an unidentified vessel, with a bunch of young boys. The last time I checked, you Terra-Marans weren't fond of traveling outside your comfortable little metro. Only Neptuan submarines roam these parts—any foreign vessels are considered threats."

I rub the spot where Gina struck me and clamber to my feet. "Well apparently we are, because as of a few hours ago, Terra-Mar is gone."

"What do you mean, *gone?*" Gina asks, her brows narrowing skeptically.

"I mean *gone*. No more, non-existent, *destroyed*."

There's only silence as all eyes stare unblinkingly at me.

"Well, that's ironic," Gina scoffs. "Because Neptua is gone, too."

Now, it's my turn to stare.

"H-how is that possible?"

"We should be asking you that," the man standing next to Gina returns quickly, narrowing his eyes suspiciously at me. "Aren't you the *Creator?* Wasn't your metro supposed to be *indestructible?*"

Under the eyes of the Neptuans and the Terra-Maran boys, I suddenly feel a long-forgotten headache coming on.

Sighing, Gina diffuses the sparks on her shock baton and clips it back onto her belt.

"We've got a lot to talk about."

CHAPTER 10

I stand at the control panel with sodden feet—my shoes are now on, but only adding to the uncomfortable moisture. This is where Gina instructed me to wait until she was ready to talk. In the entry area below, a beady-eyed man stands guard over the five boys, who he shepherded into the living quarters. Above me, the clock shows 13:30.

Before long we're met by four more Neptuan vessels, sailing in one by one and kicking up clouds of sea mud as they settle next to us on the ocean floor.

The heavy *pang* of Gina's boots echoes up the ladder, and I turn to see her emerging into the control room, her shock baton ever present on her belt.

I stuff my hands nervously into my pockets and am surprised to find the leather baseball still there. I'd completely forgotten about it amidst all the chaos.

Gina takes stock of the room, glancing quizzically at the mattress slumped in the corner and the bag of food now ripped wide and scattered across the floor. She examines each of the pressure gauges and glowing buttons on the control panel, then looks behind me at the levers and sonar screen as she passes.

With one arched brow, the woman asks, "The Liberation?"

I shrug. "Sounded good at the time."

Gina plants her hands firmly on her hips and marches toward me, stopping only inches away. From this distance, she doesn't seem quite so fearsome—the top of her head only reaches my nose. Her pale-blue eyes probe my face, clearly trying to intimidate me.

I shift uncomfortably.

"I never liked you Terra-Marans," she says. "You people were always so high and mighty about education—as if knowing everything made you capable of everything."

I stare blankly back at her, not knowing what to say. My head begins to throb again as she fingers her shock baton.

Gina turns toward the center of the floor and begins to pace, her golden ponytail swishing back and forth. She reminds me vaguely of Ruben, who did the same thing during especially passionate trains of thought.

"*Mind over matter*," she says scathingly. "That's your people's motto, isn't it? That knowledge is all humanity needs to live? That all you have to do to build something is think really hard about it, and it'll pop into existence? Well, that's not Neptua. We're much more capable of creating because we use our *hands*. We are the *true* Builders of this universe. Not you, Alan. Not you."

I stare down at the floor. I'd never realized I was such an object of resentment.

"Builders are important in Neptua," Gina continues contemplatively, still pacing. "We don't have an all-powerful Creator to give us everything we want. If we want something, we actually sweat, and *work* for it."

Returning to the center of the floor, Gina gazes up at the ceiling – her eyes darting curiously to one of the handles that I created – and inhales a deep breath.

"Then again," she says morbidly. "Neptua is gone now, so there's no point in talking about all that, is there?"

I'm silent as I watch her drop her sight back to the floor.

"How did it happen?" I ask. "The destruction of Neptua."

Gina looks slowly up at me, a troubled expression on her face. I eye her shock baton nervously, hoping I hadn't triggered a nerve, but she drops her gaze and sighs.

"That is," I add cautiously, eyeing her shock baton, "if you want to tell me."

Looking down again, she sighs.

"It was just a normal morning," she begins in a distant, reminiscent tone. "I woke up in my hut, boiled some of the fish we'd caught the night before, and headed for the submarines. The gardeners were already tending to the crops, since they wake earlier than the Transporters. In the distance, I could see that five of our ten submarines had already left to make their daily rounds delivering food to the Scatter settlement.

"When I joined my comrades, they were loading the daily rations onto our vessel. My co-captain was briefing me on the new Scatter sightings in Terra-Mar when a crack formed at the top of our enclosure. It was so small at first, barely noticeable. But then it started getting bigger and bigger, expanding over the glass like the tentacles of a giant jellyfish. Eventually, the glass broke, and the water rushed in. I watched the gardeners die instantly beneath the pressure. There was no way any of the Transporters could have helped them. They were just too far, and the water was coming in too fast. The families that were nearest the hatches were able to get into the submarines for safety. They were the lucky ones.

"I started running into my submarine along with my comrades, but halfway there I realized that my co-captain hadn't followed us. He'd gone back to try and get some of the children on the other side of the field. I called to him—told him to leave them—but it was too late. He was swallowed up in the currents, along with the children. So I ran back into my submarine and locked the hatch behind me. I radioed the other four vessels to withdraw their bridges, and we watched the ocean pulverize our beloved home."

Gina falls silent, her hands clenched into fists.

"And that's how I became captain of the last Neptuan fleet," she says bitterly. "None of us understood. Our enclosure... it was so strong... stronger than the one Terra-Mar used to have. It had never broken in the past—not even once. The only thing that could've cracked it was a submarine, but it would have had to have been big, and traveling fast. We were always so careful when operating our vessels, even the trainees. We didn't see anything when the glass started to crack."

After a pause, the woman looks wonderingly at me. "Was it the same in Terra-Mar?"

I hesitate, trying to think of the best way to answer. "I... I don't know."

Gina's brow arches higher.

"What do you mean you *don't know?*" she demands. "Your own settlement was destroyed, and you don't know how it happened?"

"I mean, when I woke up this morning, everyone was gone. Everyone except those boys. They told me that some mean-looking people made holes in our enclosure and took everyone out of the metro to their invisible submarines, then sealed the holes before they left. Nothing they said made sense, but it was my only explanation. Either that, or everyone just vanished into thin air."

"Who are those 'mean-looking people' supposed to be, anyway?" Gina asks suspiciously.

"How should I know? Like you said, only Neptuan ships roam these parts."

Gina turns away, crossing her arms over her chest. She walks to the far wall and stops there, staring at it in deep thought.

My throbbing head is now a full-on migraine. I try to distract myself by looking at the submarines outside, which glitter in front of the high beams. Through their front windows, I can vaguely see the Neptuans' outlines marching to and fro.

Nothing makes sense, I repeat hopelessly in my mind. *Nothing makes sense.*

"It must've been the Scatters," the woman finally says.

Turning around, I find Gina facing me again.

"The Scatters?" I ask. "You think the Scatters came into Terra-Mar, took the Builders, and then destroyed the metro? How could that be possible? They don't have the resources in their settlement."

"It's the only explanation I can think of," Gina says. "And let's get something straight here; the Scatters may have nothing, but they certainly don't deserve anyone's sympathy. Being a Transporter, I've seen them firsthand—they are not good people. They're violent, hateful, dangerous, and deceitful. One of them even tried to stab me with a piece of quartz when I was getting him onto my vessel. They can't be trusted or changed, Alan. They're the worst creatures in the universe!"

"Then why do we still keep them alive?" I ask, unable to contain the sympathy I'm not supposed to feel. "Once the Scatters are exiled to the Scatter settlement, they're basically useless. They aren't given any tools, or seeds to plant food, or means for catching fish to eat. They don't even have desalinaters to drink water! Why do we still keep giving them daily provisions? Why do we make them suffer? Why don't we just let them starve, or better yet, execute them?"

Gina's eyes widen in outrage.

"Because Builders don't destroy, and we definitely don't kill! Scatters destroy. Scatters kill. Builders repair, that's what we do. *We are not Scatters!*"

She looks down, her chest puffing with anger.

My head feels like it might explode from pain and rage. Keeping the Scatters alive with no means to help themselves is torture, and Gina knows it. Yet she tells me I'm not even allowed to pity them? It's unfair and unjust.

"So now what?" I ask exasperatedly. "Now that our homes are destroyed, what do we do?"

"We start over," she answers shortly. "We have Transporters, gardeners, teachers—all the right kinds of people to start anew. Only this time, *everyone* will have to contribute. We need every bit of help we can get."

Then, looking ruefully at me, she adds, "You're welcome to join us, if you want."

I stare wordlessly, considering her invitation. A metro where everyone contributes their equal share? It sounds too good to be true. I think about all the time I spent providing for the Terra-Marans—creating everything they needed, from the clothes on their backs to the enclosure that kept them safe.

And all those years working on the time machine...

It's too good to be true, I think skeptically. *A civilization where everyone carries their weight equally would never happen. The Neptuans can try to establish a place like that, but it will never last.*

"We won't ask you to create anything for us, if that's what you're worried about," Gina says, as if she could hear my thoughts. "But you can, if you want to. You can build with your hands, or with your mind. Whatever you want."

I remain silent, staring at the floor.

"Those boys," Gina says. "They need a place to grow up safely, and learn their rightful roles in civilization. That's what our new settlement will be; a place where young people can grow up to be useful, brilliant pioneers for future generations."

Her words trigger the memory of Sal, Joy, and Garrett being beaten in the docking pod.

What if I take those boys to Gina's settlement, and they eventually show Scatter traits? Will they be beaten and kidnapped, too?

Like Ruben said, people are what they are—they'll never change. That applies to the Neptuan Builders as much as it does the Scatters.

No, those boys aren't safe with the Neptuans. I can't send them away.

"Thanks for your offer," I finally answer. "But I think the boys and I are just fine where we are."

"Just fine?" Gina asks, not bothering to hide her sarcasm. "How exactly do you plan to survive?"

My head threatens to cripple me. "They think that the lost Terra-Marans are still out there, and they want to find them."

"But is searching for the lost Terra-Marans what *you* want to do?" she asks. "Or are you just searching for them because you think you owe something to those boys?"

Her question catches me off-guard. No one has ever asked me what *I* wanted to do—only what they wanted me to do for *them*.

No, searching for the lost Terra-Marans was not what I had originally wanted to do when I set out from the destroyed metro. I had wanted to go up to the surface to see that beautiful blue sky with my own eyes.

But as I look back at the woman in front of me, I realize that if I tell her the truth, she won't stop badgering me about the new settlement until I bend to her will. Just like when Ruben manipulated me into creating the time machine.

I remain quiet, and she seems to understand my decision.

Gina utters a small, "Alright, then," and turns toward the hatch to the lower level. Just before she descends through the hole, she looks back at me, her forehead wrinkled.

"You know, I remember the first time I saw you. It was four years ago, when I was still a trainee. We had just finished sending one of our own Scatters to the Scatter settlement when we received a radio call from Terra-Mar—the first one in decades, from what my older comrades told me. I remember watching from the middle of the bridge as they went into your docking pod to retrieve those Scatters. There were three of them—two Terra-Maran boys, and one girl who emigrated to your metro a few years earlier. You were crying and shouting so much that your own people had to hold you back. Your face said it all as you looked at those three Scatters being beaten. I remember thinking, 'Is that what the great and almighty Creator is? A *Scatter-sympathetic?* What kind of crazy world do we live in where our Creator loves those who destroy his creations?'"

After a thoughtful pause, she says, "Those boys… I can already tell which one of them will become a Scatter just by looking at him. It's only a matter of time before you see it, too. That is, if you live long enough."

CHAPTER 11

A little more than an hour later, Gina and her beady-eyed comrade stand in the entry area, each holding a whole dried tuna bundled in palm leaves. Beside me, the boys stare wide-eyed at the big fish, having never seen their likes before. Everyone from Terra-Mar is vegetarian, after all. With the flourishing gardens in our enclosure, we never needed to look elsewhere for nourishment.

"We figured you'd need some food for your search," the woman says. Her comrade lowers the giant fish down to Lawrence and Shawn, their short outstretched arms barely wrapping around its width. "Consider it an apology for the way we greeted you before."

At the sight of the fish, my stomach growls with hunger. I realize that I haven't eaten anything all day, and I reach out eagerly to accept her offer.

She holds the fish in front of her, but then withdraws it momentarily. "Are you absolutely sure you and the boys don't want to join us? I'm certain this won't be the last time we meet, but it will be much easier for all of us if you just accept my invitation now, while we're all here together."

I glance over at the boys—Lawrence and Shawn struggling under the tuna's weight while the others shift uncomfortably.

Whether they're Builders or Scatters, they're all safer with me.

"Thanks again, Gina, but like I said before, we're pretty committed to our search."

She gives me one last exasperated look and dumps the fish into my arms. "Suit yourself."

With a brisk turn, she heads toward the hatch, marching onto the bridge and into her submarine. The beady-eyed man turns to follow his captain, but stops to look back at me with one brow raised in a scornful expression.

"Be careful out there, *Creator*," he sniggers. "If you meet any trouble, we won't be there to protect you and your delicate little imagination."

My teeth clench. "We can hold our own, thanks."

With a smirk, he turns back to the bridge and exits The Liberation.

As soon as he passes through the opening, I tuck the fish under one arm and slam the hatch shut with the other, spinning the wheel until it locks. On the other side, the Neptuan bridge detaches from my vessel with a loud *clunk*, then whirrs as it withdraws back to its crystalline origin.

I climb up to the control room in a huff and toss the giant fish aside, the boys right on my heels. Through the enormous window, we watch the glittering vessels rock steadily back and forth, warming up their propellers. They drag forward along the seabed, sending clouds of murky soil rolling up around them as they ascend. Soon, the five Neptuan submarines are flowing away with the current of the sea, leaving The Liberation behind on the ocean floor.

My gaze wanders somberly to the screen of trickling numbers, and I press the button at the bottom, sending several clicks of sonar out into the ocean. When the image returns, I ease the engine to life, the dials of the pressure gauges quivering to show that we're stable. Before long, my submarine drags forward over the seabed, lifting up into open water.

"Why did they want us to join them?" Owen asks timidly.

I don't bother to turn around. "Don't worry about it."

The Liberation floats up almost a hundred feet before falling into pace behind the five Neptuan vessels. For some time, I drift behind them at a distance, just watching their ships glitter in my high beams. But with each passing minute, they slip farther away from me, like a school of fish that's sensed a predator. I repeatedly send out sonar, just to be sure that they're still there.

Wait, I think fleetingly. *Don't leave. Not yet.*

A twinge of regret grips me thinking about Gina's invitation. In her new settlement, I would never be expected to create anything for anyone, unless I wanted.

It would be absolutely perfect.

But then I quickly remind myself that it would only be perfect for *me*, and I had five good reasons to reject her offer.

After a few more minutes, the Neptuan submarines speed courageously ahead, disappearing into the endless abyss.

Then, a sudden *whumpf* tremors back to us, followed by a mysterious burst of light.

The Liberation shakes from the blast and we all stumble, grasping for something to hold onto.

"Whoa!"

"What was that?"

When the shaking stops, I scan the ocean outside, searching the dark horizon for anything out of the ordinary. Reaching up to the screen, I send more sonar out into the water, but when the echo returns, all I see is a cloud of loose particles scattered throughout the water.

"Isn't that where the Neptuans should be?" Owen asks.

Holding my breath, I inch a lever forward to increase The Liberation's speed. As we move closer to the cloud, a belt of glittering debris floats into view, showering the submarine with gentle rattling.

That's when the bodies drift into view—big burly ones of the Transporters, and others of men, women, and children—their tattered blue and orange robes rippling around them in the current. Their eyes are as wide open as their mouths, which gape in silent screams. Gina is among them—her golden strands now loose from her ponytail, her limbs splayed out like a starfish.

The bodies loom up to the ship nightmarishly, flipping and rolling over the glass window with quiet *plunks* as we pass through the aquatic graveyard.

In my head I see the face of the baby from the Mars colony. I see him cradled in the arms of his father—the man whose name I never knew. I hear the adoring words of his mother—the woman whose face I never saw. I remember the hordes of screaming people as the Mars colony burst into bits, their blood vaporizing into the atmosphere like pink clouds, their bodies speckling the emerald-green grass like clamshells smashed upon deep-sea rocks.

Fear erupts in my chest and I slam the lever forward to race away from the carnage. I want to find out what happened, but at the same time, I want to forget.

"W-what happened to them?" Shawn asks shakily.

"Are they...Are they..."

Dead. The Neptuans are *dead.*

Just like the people on the Mars colony, every trace of the Neptuans was destroyed—their submarines, their people, their futures—scattered into the vast and infinite ocean.

It's not just a video this time.

This is all real.

"Who would do such a thing?" Owen gapes.

In the farthest reaches of the high beams, a massive glittering outline materializes into view. It's saucer-like in shape, and wider than all the crystalline Neptuan submarines combined. Its spiky edges twirl menacingly as it glides toward us.

And that's when, for the first time, I feel an emotion I thought was reserved for Scatters.

Rage.

Pure, hot, flaming rage, like I want to destroy everything in my path.

"What *is* that thing?" Cal asks.

"I have no idea," I snarl back, my eyes locked ahead. "But I'm pretty sure it's what killed the Neptuans."

Locking my hands onto the controls, I nosedive toward the sea floor, daring the enigma to follow. The boys howl and shriek, clawing at the floor to stay in place. Everything around them slides to the front of the ship and clatters noisily into a heap.

Through the front window, the flat barrier of the ocean floor looms up at me.

"What are you doing?!" Shawn yells.

"We're going to crash!"

Fury surges through my veins. "That thing destroyed humanity's best chance of survival. Now *I'm* going to destroy *it!*"

Only a few feet above the muddy soil, I yank the lever backward, pulling The Liberation upright. The metal groans as we level out—just in time to save us from a watery grave. Clatters sound behind me as the objects in the front of the ship tumble back onto the floor, followed by a series of *Oofs!* and *Ows!* from the boys. Keeping my hands firmly grasped on the levers, I direct the submarine forward, skidding over the seabed recklessly.

From the waters outside, a muffled *whumpf* confirms that the enigma followed us—and just crashed into the ocean floor.

Gotcha!

I swerve The Liberation around to inspect the damage. The

crash-landed enigma is in my sight—or at least I think it is. The high beams only illuminate a rolling cloud of dirt around it.

"Bastard!" I growl. "Show yourself!"

As if hearing my thoughts, the enigma shudders, sending more clouds billowing up around it.

"Get back up and face me, dammit!" My hands grip the levers as if they were triggers to guns. "I dare you! I'll kill you like you killed those innocent Neptuans! *Come on!*"

"Alan..." Owen gasps from somewhere behind me. "How can you say that? Would you really kill someone?"

But I ignore him. This is more than the timid boy can understand. That *thing* killed our last hope for humanity. Of course I would do the same to whoever was operating it to avenge the Neptuans' deaths.

That person deserves to die.

And then, as mysteriously as it appeared, the enigma vanishes—just like the lost Terra-Marans.

I gape at the baffling emptiness, the high beams once again shining into nothing but darkness.

"Are we safe now?" Lawrence whispers.

I don't know. A part of me hopes so, but the other part of me wants the enigma to return so I can get another chance to attack it.

But after five, ten, fifteen more minutes of glaring into the infinite sea, I finally admit that it's gone.

Our only clue to finding the Terra-Marans is gone.

CHAPTER 12

I sit alone on the floor of the control room, wallowing in my moment of misery. It was almost 3:30 when I turned the engine off, plunging The Liberation into a deathly silence, and I'm not sure how much time has passed since then. I just stare helplessly out the window, fingering the baseball and remembering the horror of the bodies floating past the ship.

From the living quarters I can hear the boys gobbling away at the dried tuna—their first meal since our home was destroyed.

How could they eat at a time like this? I think angrily, tightening my grip on the baseball. *Our home is gone, and so is Neptua. We still have no idea where the lost Terra-Marans are, and we just lost our only clue to their whereabouts. Kids are so ignorant.*

Through my troubled thoughts, I vaguely feel my stomach gurgle. But I ignore it, focusing instead on my despair. All at once I feel alone, confused, and angry.

I should've never created this damn thing, I think dejectedly, glaring down at the baseball. It was what started everything—Terra-Mar's insatiable hunger to model itself after the glorious metros of the past; Garrett, Joy, and Sal's exile to the Scatter settlement; the emergence of new Scatters in Terra-Mar; and now, my being stuck down here at the bottom of the ocean, halfway to hell.

In a fit of rage, I thrust the baseball at the foot of the control panel, where it slams against the metal with a sharp *pong* and ricochets somewhere to the back of the room.

I bury my face in my hands, moaning despondently. Within the darkness of my mind, I see the destruction of the Mars colony again—the explosions threatening to rip me apart and bury me beneath the rusty-red Martian soil like they did the poor people there.

They were good people—good *Builders*. They should have lived.

That baby and his parents shouldn't have died on Mars.

And the Neptuans shouldn't have died under the oceans of Earth.

Guilt spreads through me like a virus. I lean back against the chair, blinking away tears.

"I'm such a coward," I croak, my throat tightening with sorrow. "I'm a weak, useless coward who can't build with his hands. I don't even care about the people I'm supposed to protect."

Ruben would be so ashamed of me now. He would tell me that I'm nothing like the great pioneer of humanity's future that he taught me to be.

I'm just a useless coward.

Coward, *coward, COWARD!*

Footsteps *ping* softly up the ladder, and I quickly wipe the tears from my eyes. A few seconds later, Owen's shy sapphire eyes gaze curiously up at me.

"Hey, Alan, thought you might need some company." He moves to sit next to me on the floor, where he crosses his legs and slumps forward to prop his head up in his palms.

I don't respond to the young boy, keeping my eyes fixed on the window instead. I'm not at all in the mood to talk with him, but I resist the urge to shoo him away, simply because I know that he'll be sensitive about it.

For a few seconds, the two of us sit silently—him staring down at the floor while I stare out into the ocean at the spot where the enigma disappeared.

"I think I'm a Scatter," Owen says.

He doesn't seem bothered by the statement. I look at him to find a blank, even bored expression on his face.

"I never contributed anything to Terra-Mar," he explains. "And my teachers always said that I didn't pay attention. They told me that if I didn't start learning faster, I'd stray behind everyone else—that I wouldn't be able to carry on the knowledge of humanity. They were all calling me a Scatter without actually saying it."

I look back to the ocean, Gina's words echoing through my head. *I already know which one will be a Scatter.*

Focusing back on the ocean, I think wearily, *So this is the boy that Gina was talking about. Timid, soft-spoken Owen is the Scatter.*

The two of us then fall back into our routine of silence – him staring down at the floor, and I, staring out at the ocean.

"Well, that doesn't matter anymore," I sigh bitterly. "The Neptuans are gone, so there won't be anyone to drag you off to the Scatter Settlement, and all of human civilization is destroyed, so there's no use for Builders anymore, either. You're perfectly safe now."

Perfectly safe to just sit here, and rot to death.

"But there's something I never understood about Scatters," Owen continues. "They're all supposed to be violent and brutal—breaking things and hurting others. I don't think I'm violent, I'm very careful at everything I do, and I certainly don't like hurting people. I don't feel like a Scatter at all; more like something *between* a Builder and a Scatter. Something like..."

Owen pauses as he tries to find the right word.

"... a *Neutral*."

I blink hard. A Neutral? People who don't build, or destroy, but who simply, I suppose, *coexist* with them?

In the few hours I've known Owen, he's never once done or said anything that displayed the pride of the Builders, or the supposed violence of the Scatters.

I've never heard of a Neutral before, but it almost makes sense.

Then, my heart jumps. *Could Garrett have been one, also? A Neutral?*

"They're still out there, Alan," the timid boy reassures. "The lost Terra-Marans... I just have this feeling that they're still out there, waiting for us to bring back the civilization that was stolen from them. I know that our situation seems hopeless now, but the other boys and I believe that you can set everything back in place again. We know all about the burdens that you've carried for the metro, and we admire you for that."

I know he means well, but I can feel outrage bubbling within me. How could a bunch of little boys know what carrying a burden feels like?

Owen's cheeks redden with embarrassment. "In our classes, they asked us what we wanted to be, if we could choose. Everyone said they wanted to be the Creator."

I hang my head at his words. I would never wish the lonely role of Creator on anyone—not for all the knowledge and glory in the universe. Owen and his friends only saw the grandeur behind my suffering.

"We know that you can make everything right, Alan," he says, glancing hopefully over at me. "You've revived civilization down here in the bottom of the ocean once—you can surely do it again. You're the Creator. You can bring *anything* into existence."

Again I feel the outrage tighten in my chest. How can Owen be so impossibly optimistic when he just watched practically all of humanity die before his eyes? There's no one left to civilize this planet. There is no hope for any of us down here.

Owen pushes himself up from the floor. "But if you really don't want to do this anymore, you're better off just creating a separate submarine for the five of us. At least then, we'd all be happy going our own ways, doing what we want to do."

With that, he scurries off down the ladder and back to his friends.

I stare after him, stunned at his intuition. Is that what Neutrals are? People who understand others without asking?

Across the room, I notice the baseball lying in the corner. I walk over and pick it up, raising it up to the light to examine. Even after all these years, it's like new—every detail I bestowed upon it that fateful day in Ruben's class still unchanged.

I remember the first time I actually *used* it—when I played catch with Garrett, my best friend. I was so happy in that moment, probably the happiest I've ever been.

That is, until this morning, when I ran blissfully through the deserted locales, free of the usual crowds, and especially free of my ever-watchful teacher.

But why was I not abducted along with the other Terra-Marans? I suddenly wonder. I've been so wracked with adrenaline this whole day, this is the first time I've actually stopped to question my survival. Owen and the other boys hid in a part of the metro that was not designated for living or learning, but I was in my pod all along. The abductors could have taken me, but they chose not to.

What's more, the enclosure didn't start to collapse until I was awake and prepared to exit.

Did I just get extremely lucky, or had the abductors actually *wanted* me to escape?

Stuffing the baseball back into my pocket, I turn and leap toward the ladder, climbing hurriedly down to the puddled entry area. The hatch to the living quarters stands a few inches ajar, and I swing it open to find the boys staring quizzically up at me from the two bottom bunk beds, bits of tuna in their mouths.

"Alright," I huff. "Let's figure out who those mean-looking people were. Did they look old? Young? What were they wearing? Give me details."

"Some were old," Shawn mumbles through a bite of fish.

"And some were young," Owen joins in. "The youngest looked maybe a few years older than us."

"Go on, go on." I pace back and forth in the small space, the way Ruben used to.

"They had pieces of metal on their bodies, like armor."

"Some of them wore Terra-Maran clothes."

"And others wore old robes that were blue and orange."

It can't be, I think dreadfully. *It can't be them. It's impossible. How could they have gotten into the metro?*

"That's what the older Terra-Marans wore before I created the levels of the Metro," I explain. "None of you were born yet, so you wouldn't remember. What else did you see?"

"They had shock batons, like the Neptuans," Beckett offers.

I gulp. That didn't bode well. "What about names? Did anyone call to each other?"

"Oh, yeah! They did!" Owen says energetically, wriggling out from under the fish in his lap. "One of them was named Perry!"

Cal nods. "I heard a few names, too. I think they were Saunders, and Katherine."

"Do any of those sound familiar to you, Alan?"

My brows stitch together, trying to remember, but I come up short. "No, never heard of 'em."

"There were also these two other names," Beckett says. "I can't be sure, but they sounded like *Joy* and *Sal*."

I halt immediately.

My friends.

If Joy and Sal were in the metro this morning, then Garrett must have been there, too. How did they get out of the Scatter settlement?

Were the rest of the kidnappers Scatters too?

Throughout Terra-Mar's history, people have blamed the Scatters for practically every calamity—humanity's fall from the stars, the squalor conditions within the old enclosure, even the soil's lack of growth.

I've lived my whole life trying to believe that the Scatters were simply misunderstood, but I can't ignore the evidence in front of me.

"So the Scatters are behind all of this," I whisper, my eyes dropping to the floor. "I don't know how they got out of their settlement, but I guess the better question is... *why* did they do it? Why did they come to Terra-Mar and take the Builders?"

For the first time, the boys are all silent.

Then, Owen shrugs. "I guess we'll just have to go the Scatter settlement and find out."

CHAPTER 13

From what people have told me, the route to the Scatter settlement is dangerous and complex, full of mindboggling underwater caverns and tunnels.

At first, we glide effortlessly through miles of smooth water, but then we descend into the jagged valleys and canyons.

For the next twenty-four hours, I guide us through the narrow passages, constantly eyeing the threatening darkness and releasing sonar clicks to ensure that our path is clear. My hands grip the control levers shakily, steering The Liberation clear of the sharply jutting stones around it. When I'm tired to the point of collapse, I show the boys how to operate the vessel, being as meticulous as possible despite the sleep deprivation. To my relief, they take to their duties with strict caution, and I finally retire to the living quarters.

We finish the scraps of the fish carcasses quickly, and now only have the powdery remains of the dried vegetables to sustain us. We need to find the Scatter settlement soon or we'll starve.

....

At the end of the second day, I'm back in the control room while the boys take a break to nap. My belly growls with hunger—the last time I ate was hours ago, and even then it was barely a mouthful. Determined to reach the Scatter settlement as quickly as possible, I lean forward against the control panel, pressing The Liberation ever onward.

Eventually I emerge into a wide clearing, where the sides of the stone drop deep down into a crevasse beneath me. I release a long exhale, thankful that I no longer have to squeeze through all those tight spaces.

A few meters ahead, I catch sight of what look like angelic glowing droplets hanging motionless in the water.

What are those things? I wonder, squinting at them. *Fish? Plankton?*

As The Liberation approaches, I send out sonar to see if I can get a reading. What echoes back is a veil of radiance that paints the screen gold, like a halo.

For a moment, I worry that the hunger has gotten to me and I've started seeing things. But after several hard blinks, the lights are still there. I press the button again, sending out another few clicks of sonar.

This time the response is an enchanting sound—both haunting and serene—like a blue whale calling longingly across the vast stretches of the sea. It resonates in the water, seeping through The Liberation's hull and caressing my ears. It trickles through them and into my very being.

Though I try to resist it, I feel myself lulled into a kind of trance, and I close my eyes, indulging in the refuge of my mind. I envision myself coaxed out of my own body—transported to a place where there is no time; where my imagination is all that exists.

There, something—or some*one*—tells me that I'm safe, that I will be saved.

It feels familiar somehow, as if it's been with me all along, but this is the first time I'm actually hearing it.

The voice assures that it will always be near—that it will never leave me, not even at the end of my life. Not even at the end of everything.

Clink, clink, clink.

My eyes flutter open to see the last of the glowing droplets bounce off the front window and tumble down into the unreachable depths of the crevasse beneath. In the distance ahead, the entrance to yet another narrow tunnel looms into view.

Snapping out of my trance, I grab the lever from where it veered off-kilter and aim the bow into the opening. Glancing fleetingly out of the right window, I utter a disappointed, "Oh…" as the last of the droplets disappear.

Chapter 14

The older Terra-Marans always told me horrible stories about the Scatter settlement—about the pain, rage, and despair of the people who were sent there, never to leave. They described it as a man-made hell—no light, very little food besides the rations that the Neptuans threw to them during their daily feedings, and no form of air ventilation whatsoever. Anyone who arrived there died shortly afterward from starvation or illness.

After six hours of maneuvering through the narrow tunnel, The Liberation emerges into a wide valley. The mountain to either side of us expands outward from the ocean floor, then grows narrowly together again overhead, making it utterly impossible to enter from above.

By now, the boys are awake, and I supervise them at their posts—Shawn at the levers, Beckett standing atop a steel chair at the sonar screen, Lawrence at the right window, Owen at the left, and Cal at the wall of buttons. Together, we gaze ahead at the colossal structure that looms up to us.

The Scatter settlement appears to be ten times the size of Terra-Mar, and is wedged tightly between the two mountainsides like a creature trapped in a great white shark's teeth. From behind the darkened glass, intermittent sparks of electricity reveal glimpses of a puzzling infrastructure within. Three hatches line the enclosure's base, marking the entrances where the Neptuans deliver food, while two more line the other side, where the seabed drops sharply down to a gorge. Dotting the mountainsides around the settlement, the rudders of long-dormant hydro turbines glint in the far-reaching brilliance of The Liberation's high beams.

Apparently the Scatters weren't always without power.

This prison is the largest human invention after our fall from the stars. Not Neptua. Not Terra-Mar. But the Scatter settlement.

A chill runs up my spine as I try to imagine what could possibly survive inside there, but I quickly drop the thought.

Shawn brings a lever gently forward, tipping The Liberation down toward the ocean floor, where it then glides cautiously toward the settlement.

"Cal, turn off the lights," I whisper, as if whatever is hiding inside the soul-chilling enclosure can hear me.

Obediently, Cal flips a toggle, and the lights in and around the submarine vanish, plunging us into the ocean's darkness. Now there's nothing to guide us toward the Scatter settlement except the strange electrical sparks within it. The trickling green radiance of the sonar screen is the only source of light in the control room.

For a few tense minutes, we drift silently through the deep water, Shawn inching the lever slowly backward to slow the vessel. When we are only a few feet away, he tilts the submarine gently until its hatch aligns with the one at the enclosure's center.

"I'm going to dock The Liberation on the seabed so Cal can extend the bridge to the settlement," Shawn announces. He turns to the left window, where Cal nods cooperatively, already poising one hand over the appropriate button.

"No, wait," I say, holding a halting hand out to both of them. "The Scatters are expecting us to come to them. They have harmful intentions, remember? We can't just walk in through the front door, we have to create our own way inside."

There, I said it, I think disappointedly. *I said that the Scatters had harmful intentions. Now, I'm just like everybody else.*

Pushing the thought aside, I lower myself to one knee and press my palms against the floor, imagining a tunnel that will dig into the ocean floor and burrow past the borders of the nightmarish settlement.

The familiar warming sensation surges down my body, into my arms and legs. Soon, the ridges of a rectangular hatch form in the floor, with a small wheel lock to open it.

I spin the wheel until it unlocks and flip the hatch open, only to hear a cacophony of muffled voices swelling out from the tunnel I created.

The boys gather around me uncertainly, fear glowing in their eyes as the sound washes over us. I want to tell them that I'm scared too, but instead I grit my teeth and crouch down to the opening.

The metal of the ladder feels like ice beneath my fingers, which I suppose makes sense, since the temperature at this level of the sea is just above freezing.

I'm only a few steps down before I hear the, *ping, ping, ping* of the boys' footsteps above me. Nearing the bottom of the ladder, I release my grip and jump down to the tunnel floor, but I misjudge the distance and hit the ground with a loud *PANG.* A sharp pain streaks up my right leg.

"Ah!" I grunt, dropping to my knee.

I clutch my ankle, which is surely sprained.

"Be quiet, Alan," Lawrence calls down to me.

"The Scatters might hear us," Owen agrees.

Guiding my hand against the freezing wall of the tunnel, I pull myself back to standing and wince at the pain when I try to put weight on my foot.

I attempt to limp forward in the darkness, but with my slowed pace, the boys catch up quickly. For several long minutes, the six of us travel wordlessly in the dark, rubbing our hands against our sleeves to stay warm. The muffled voices grow louder, but no more discernible—I try unsuccessfully to make out their words.

Somehow I know that they're not saying anything pleasant.

The Terra-Marans must be here, I think anxiously. There's nowhere else for them to go.

By the time I arrive at the end of the tunnel, the voices are so loud that my ears begin to ring. Feeling along the wall in front of me, I find another ladder and climb slowly upward, exhaling laboriously whenever I have to step on my right ankle. Before long, my head touches a flat barrier above me, and I raise my hand to it, pushing it gently open.

As soon as I lift the hatch, my ears flood with the now crystal clear cries of the anguished voices.

Somebody, please help me!

I can't take this anymore!

Kill me, please! Kill me now and end my suffering!

They're losing their minds, I think, my heart racing with shock. *The Terra-Marans are losing their minds here in the dark.*

That's when the stench wafts into my nostrils—it's like rotting meat mixed with the sickly sweetness of pineapples. It wrings my stomach like a wet rag, and I feel the remains of last night's fish dinner fight its way back up.

Swallowing hard, I climb out from the tunnel in time for a startling burst of electricity to explode in my face. I yelp and cower back down, dropping the barrier shut above me.

"What's going on up there?"

"What did you see, Alan?"

With shallow breath, I chance another peek at the settlement, emerging slowly to see the electric sparks now coming from a few feet away in the dirt. Several paces past those, more sparks spout from the ground, and overhead there's a hanging veil of them, swaying like seaweed in the waves.

The stench is overwhelming, but I focus on breathing through my mouth as I step out from the tunnel, careful not to apply too much pressure onto my right ankle. I can practically feel the hopelessness of the people here, crawling around in the dark, howling for their lives.

With so many people screaming for help, I fear I won't be able to even identify the Terra-Marans, let alone get them past the Scatters and into The Liberation.

Suddenly, something grabs the back of my sweater and drags me to the right.

"Let go of me!" I yell, flailing against the arm that's holding onto me. "Don't touch me, you bastard, let go!"

I wrestle and scratch, my ankle burning with pain, but no matter what I do, the grip of this phantom-like entity is too strong to break. I scream at the top of my lungs, gulping down lungfuls of the putrid air, but to no avail.

Stumbling over something hard and round, I bend and grab what feels like a rock and thrust it over my shoulder at my abductor. A man's cry of pain sounds from behind, and the grip on me finally releases.

Falling backward onto the floor, I scramble as fast as I can on my hands and knees in the direction from where I was taken. Through the terrain of sparks in front of me, I try to identify the outline of the hatch, but the blackness of this shadowy hell makes it impossible for me to see anything.

My heart racing in my chest, I stumble to my feet and start to run despite my screaming ankle. It's an endless labyrinth of sizzling sparks, and I pant against the foul decaying air. I run, and run, and run, listening to the agonized voices around me.

Somebody, anybody!

I don't want to live like this anymore!

The voices invade my ears, clawing into my brain. Their agony is relentless.

"Ahhh!" I begin to scream along with them, clutching my head. "Get out of my head! Get out of my mind! Get me out of here, somebody!"

I've only been here for a few minutes, and this place is already ripping me apart sense by sense. How could we have made this settlement such a cruel, vile place?

Soon my ankle gives out, and I tumble forward onto the dirt with a labored, *Oomph!* A spark of light bursts near my face, illuminating a human skull that grins toothily at me, its two hollow sockets glaring straight into my eyes.

"Ahhh!" I shriek again, clambering desperately away from the remains of the long-dead Terra-Maran or Neptuan. Never in my whole life could I imagine a place as appalling and horrifying as this.

As I crawl backward, one hand hits open air and I cry in alarm, scrambling around to peer at the ditch I'd almost fallen into. It explodes with a cascade of sparks, momentarily illuminating a pile of bodies clothed in Terra-Maran and Neptuan outfits. They lie haphazardly on top of each other, their pale faces gaping upward at some false salvation.

These people are all dead.

With horror, I catch sight of two familiar faces—a woman with whom I share my freckles, and a man with whom I share my dirty-blonde hair. Their hands are linked together, even now.

Even in death.

I fall instantly silent. All the horrors of the Scatter settlement can't compare to what I feel now.

They're never coming back.

All the time I put them second so that I could focus on creation—I'll never get that back.

All the time in the lab—gone.

My parents are dead.

They're never coming back.

My parents are dead.

My parents are dead.

An eerie sound escapes from my throat, like choking at first, but then it ruptures into something completely foreign. An unrecognizable emotion wells up inside me. I feel every cell in my body burn with a sharp, clawing desire—a desire to do unto the Scatters what they've done to their victims. To cause them as much pain, fear, and suffering as they caused the Builders they murdered.

I want revenge.

The attacker returns, grabbing me by the collar again and dragging me away again.

It's him, I think as I rip at the hand that holds me. Rage slithers out of my chest, like an eel rearing to strike. *He took my parents away from me.*

"You did it, didn't you?" I shriek, tossing in his grip. "You killed my parents, and all the other Builders! You filthy Scatter! You deserve to rot down here!"

Somebody, please help me!

I can't take this anymore!

Kill me! I don't want to live like this anymore! Please kill me now, and end my suffering!

"You did it, didn't you?!" I continue hollering while still inflicting my blows at his arm. "Why don't you just say it, huh? Why don't you admit what you killed them! Aren't you proud of what you did? Aren't you proud of killing all those people?!"

Just kill me, please!

I can't take it anymore!

"Why can't you say it, huh?" I screech. "Why can't you admit what you did? You killed those people, and you liked doing it. Say it! SAY IT, DAMMIT!"

I anchor my left foot firmly into the ground, and lean away from my abductor's pull.

Somebody!

Please, help!

Kill me! Kill me now!

"SAY THAT YOU KILLED THEM!" I bellow, elbowing wildly against the man. "ADMIT THAT YOU DID IT! DID IT MAKE YOU HAPPY TO TAKE THEIR LIVES, YOU FILTHY, EVIL, DISGUSTING SCAT—"

"Stop, Alan, stop," a familiar voice hisses from the darkness. The grip loosens from my sweater. "It's only me."

He reaches down and closes a hand around one of the sparks, raising the wire from which it spouts up to illuminate his face—two copper-brown eyes behind a pair of cracked rectangular glasses.

It's Ruben.

CHAPTER 15

"I knew it was you when I saw that light outside the enclosure!" Ruben says as he leads me hobbling to the far edge of the settlement. The wire still sizzles radiantly in his other hand. "When I saw it, I thought to myself, 'The Creator has come to save us! My dear student has come to save his teacher!'"

Stopping at one of the mountain bases, Ruben releases my arm and lowers himself to the ground. There, the light from the wire reveals three ashen youths huddling in the cold—one is a brown-skinned Transporter, and the other two are Belinda and Chad, their exhales creating puffs of steam.

"A-Alan," Chad whispers through chattering teeth. "Is that y-you?"

"Not so loud," the blue-eyed girl hushes him. "The Scatters will know she's here." Her normally coral-pink lips are now a deep purple.

Somebody!

Please, help!

Kill me! Kill me now!

I lower myself carefully to their level. "What's going on here?"

"When the Scatters took us, they threw us in here with the Neptuans and dared us to try and stay alive for as long as we could. It was so cold and dark—we had no idea what they were going to do to us. So some of the Builders pushed back, and then... and then..."

And then they were killed, I finish gravely in my mind, recalling the bodies in the ditch.

The anguished cries of the Scatter prisoners continue to wail in the background.

Fixing his hazel eyes on me, the young Transporter sputters, "My crewmembers were supposed to be coming for us during the daily feeding rounds. Did you see them? Do they know what happened to us?"

I nod tragically. "Yes, I saw them, and they told me that Neptua has been destroyed. Not long after that, they were attacked by..." I pause, collecting myself. "...something. I'm sorry, but they're all gone."

The Transporter blinks in disbelief. "Gina too? The captain?"

I nod my head dismally, then turn back to my friends. "Terra-Mar was destroyed, too. It happened after you were all taken."

"Dammit!" Ruben curses through clenched teeth. "They took everything from us, and now they're taking our very lives. They're the ones who deserve to die—those worthless Scatters!"

I can't agree more.

Because of the Scatters, I will never see my parents again.

I hate the Scatters.

I want them dead.

My teacher looks pleadingly to me in the sizzling light, his free hand clutching my shoulder.

"You have to get us out of here, Alan," he wheezes, leaning in close to me. His breath smells strangely of dirt, even urine. I wonder grotesquely if that was what he's been drinking since there was no water in the Scatter settlement. "You have to take us away from this place before *he* comes down again!"

Somebody!

Please, help!

Kill me! Kill me now!

"Who's *he?*" I ask, dreading the answer. "Who are you afraid of?"

"Alan!" a small voice suddenly shouts from somewhere in the tormented clamor. "Alan, where are you? Where'd you go?"

Oh no, the boys! I think in panic. I'd forgotten all about them. *They're going to give us away!*

"Alan!"

"Where are you, Alan?"

"Don't leave us!"

"Alan!"

A grid of fluorescent lamps bursts alight far above us. The anguished voices halt immediately, and the electric sparks disappear.

I shield my eyes instinctively from the unexpected brightness, feeling suddenly exposed. When I ease them open again, I can actually see the Scatter settlement for the first time.

The terrain is littered with the bones of long-deceased Scatters, along with pieces of decaying fruits and vegetables. Cowering among them are the lost Terra-Maran and Neptuan builders, their clothing stained with blood and filth. A few feet away from me stands a forest of black diamond columns rising from the ground to support a maze of bridges, platforms, and staircases that wind dramatically up to the top of the enclosure.

This place, I think with a mixture of awe and revulsion. *Its infrastructure is even bigger than Terra-Mar's. It's even* better *than Terra-Mar's.*

So this is where everyone is.

I've finally found the lost Builders.

A tiny figure leaps out from the highest platform and speeds to the ground like a missile.

"It's *him!*" the Builders howl in fright, pointing dreadfully up at the man. "Everyone, hide!"

The figure lands in a bath of shockwaves, the impact scooping a crater into the earth. It sucks the very breath out of the unfortunate bodies caught within its perimeter, leaving them rigid and lifeless.

Did he just kill them? I think in horror, watching the luckier Builders around the crater disperse in pandemonium.

As he emerges onto the ledge of the crater, I get a clearer view of the man—his expression is sunken, his chin covered in a bristly gray beard. He wears glinting metal cuffs on both wrists, and a thick silver helmet on his head. He hoists himself above the earth and plants two booted feet sturdily into the ground.

So this is a Scatter... This is what the Builders have hated and feared for generations.

He raises his arms above his head and slams his fists onto the ground with a resounding *WHOOMPH,* sending another shockwave burrowing through the dirt toward me at an impossible speed.

My companions and I dive out of its way, leaving the force to slam into the mountainside behind us. Pebbles fly into the air and rain down on our heads.

Shielding my eyes, I gape at the terrifying creature.

How did he do that?

"Hey, Perry!" a nasally voice calls from the top platform. "What're you getting so excited about? They're just *Builders!* All they do is *die.* They're no fun!"

Rotating his head eerily upward, Perry growls in a deep guttural tone, "Why don't you get down here and see for yourself, Saunders?"

A second figure springs nimbly down, his blue and orange robe flapping around him. He lands beside the crater with an ear-splitting *BOOM* that vibrates throughout the settlement. The ground shudders in response, as if the very tectonic plates are shifting beneath us. Cries ring out around me as a second shockwave slices through the air in my direction.

Digging my shoes into the dirt (and wincing from the pain of my ankle), I thrust myself out of the way just before the shockwave collides with the mountainside, slicing a wedge-shaped cut into it.

"So this is the great *Creator*, huh?" Saunders muses, a nefarious smirk on his cracked lips. He looks perhaps thirty-three or thirty-four, and he wears the same armor as Perry. The bottom of his robe is too short to conceal his scrawny legs, which are covered in curly, rust-colored hair. The only vulnerable part of him is his feet—bare like the Terra-Marans' were before the metro was formed.

And his eyes... they're the most revolting eyes I've ever seen—plagued with gangrenous spots and gushing with puss along the sides.

Glancing over at his fellow Scatter, Saunders muses, "He doesn't look so tough to me. What do you think, Perry?"

My heart pounds with alarm as Perry's hardened expressions twists into a loathsome scowl. "Let's make him wish he was never born!"

Before I can react, he raises his arms and slams his fists down on the ground again, sending another shockwave charging toward me.

I scramble to my feet and limp as fast as I can toward the far edge of the settlement, Saunders' maniacal cackle following me the entire way, *HEH, HEH, HEH!*

A group of Builders divide as I approach, revealing three tiny hatches behind them.

I jump out of the shockwave's trajectory just in time for it to smash a hole in the glass and send freezing ocean water cascading inside.

Oh no! I think in panic. *If the Scatters don't kill us, the ocean surely will!*

But then, as fast as it broke, the glass smooths over with a new layer, sealing the water back into the frigid depths.

"Huh?" I utter confusedly. How did the enclosure just repair itself like that?

With a rush of wind, Saunders leaps high into the air, his eyes fixed on me.

Anticipating another attack, I throw myself toward the dispersing flock of Builders, but I can't move fast enough. Behind me, the *BOOM* of Saunders' landing shudders the terrain, knocking me agonizingly onto my belly.

"I thought you were supposed to be all-powerful, Creator!" Saunders taunts giddily.

When the shuddering stops, I push myself relentlessly back to my feet and dart toward the base of the mountain on the other side. A sheen of sweat forms over my skin, making the freezing air rushing by me feel even colder.

Glancing fearfully over one shoulder, I see Saunders stomp one bare foot onto the ground, sending yet another shockwave toward me. It sprays dirt aside as it goes.

Losing my balance, I tumble forward onto the soil again, feeling my very skeleton throttle upon impact. But the shockwave fast approaches, and I know I won't be able to escape this one.

I need to protect myself somehow.

I fling my arms up instinctively in defense, feeling them burn like fire as what I assume is the shockwave finally hits me. I hold my breath and wait for the end, but to my astonishment, I open my eyes to find a shield of sparkling clear diamond – the hardest naturally occurring material on this planet – around me, stopping the shockwave in its path until it dissipates to a mere gust of wind.

"Woo hoo, look at that, Perry!" Saunders laughs, his fractured outline jumping gleefully through the haze of the diamond shield. "The little Creator is finally showing his stuff. What fun!"

My hands feel like fire, and I wave them back and forth to try to cool them. But I don't have time to rest, because Perry sends his own bone-rattling *WHOOMPH* a moment later.

There's nowhere to run. I'm cornered.

I can't believe I didn't see this before, I think, the sweat now running down my forehead. *This is all a trap. The Scatter settlement is a trap to get me killed!*

With the shockwave rushing toward me and nowhere to escape, I have no choice but to do something I've never had to do before – fight back for my life.

Aiming my palm out at the Scatter, I clench my eyes shut and think as hard as I can about more glittering diamond shards shooting from my hand. To my relief, I feel my fingertips scorch as a cloud of sparkling brilliance bursts out from them, neutralizing the sonic current and pelting Perry in the face.

The older Scatter stumbles backward in surprise, slapping the shards off of him. I expect him to retaliate, but instead he looks up at the platforms angrily. "Katherine! Can't you see we need help? Get down here already!"

A woman's voice, low and scratchy, yells back, "Oh, *now* you want my help? What happened to me being a useless old hag yesterday, huh?"

"Just get down here already, you stupid bitch!"

From one of the middle platforms, a broad-shouldered figure in a faded robe just like Saunders' crawls from the shadows, curly blonde hair peeking out from beneath her helmet.

When she catches sight of me, she scoffs. "You're telling me two big strong men can't handle a little boy?!" Katherine scoffs down.

She swings one fist over her head, the metal cuff on her wrist glinting in the light, and strikes the column next to her, producing a spiky cluster of black diamonds. They explode from the column with an unsettling *CRACK* and rocket to the ground, smashing against the earth and charging toward me.

My eyes bulge in fright and I thrust my palms in front of me, feeling them sear like hot metal as two trails of clear jagged diamonds skewer up from the dirt. They crash against the woman's attack in glimmering shards.

Perry and Saunders are running at me now, no longer bothering with the sonic attacks.

On impulse, I dive forward into the shady forest of columns, where I collapse onto my hands and knees, panting. I reach shakily down and lift my pant leg to discover my ankle now swollen to the size of a small beet.

"Dammit!" I curse, placing my palm over the swell. I can feel my racing pulse beneath the bulging skin. I won't be able to run for much longer.

Without warning, an ear-splitting *SMASH* sends the columns shuddering around me. A circle of spikes opens in the platform directly overhead, and Katherine's flushed face pokes through, her mud-brown eyes locking deviously onto me.

"It's all your fault that we're here!" she shrieks, droplets of sooty-hued

plaque spitting out from her deteriorating teeth. "*You're the reason we're here!*"

With the flick of her wrist, she sends the spikes around her shooting down at me like venomous stingers.

In a panic, I swipe my arm across the air in front of me, creating a bouquet of bright clear crystals that shatter against hers. The Scatter woman tumbles backward from the impact, her feet kicking wildly. She screams an enraged, "AHHH!" as she falls.

I struggle to my feet while she's down, but the moment I put pressure on my mangled ankle, I crumble back to the dirt, whimpering in pain. Soil gets in my mouth as I cry out, filling it with an acrid, mineral taste. By the time I'm upright again, Perry and Saunders have almost completely gained on me.

This is it, I think. *This is where the Scatters take my life. This is where they win.*

I close my eyes against welling tears, but somebody yanks me up by my collar and drags me backward, nearly choking me. I watch as another blast of black crystals slices past the spot where I lay, and hear Katherine's aggravated shouts from somewhere in the columns. She emerges briefly through a gap in the iron and I see her clutching her face as if someone had thrown something at her.

After we've moved a safe distance away, my savior releases his grip and I fall limply to the dirt. Tilting my head backward, I find the brown-skinned Transporter from before, a distraught expression on his face.

"We need to fight back, Creator!" he pleads. "This has to end now!"

I glance back to the shade of the columns, where Perry, Saunders, and Katherine all gather—waiting. Their armor seems to glow, as if I can *see* them regaining their energy.

"The metal," I realize, looking earnestly back to the Transporter. "They're using their armor as some sort of energy magnifier. If we want to beat them, we need to get it off."

The Transporter nods. "Alright, I'll get my crew, and you'll bait the Scatters toward us."

"Wait, *I'm BAIT?!*" I exclaim, but he's already up and running before I can protest. He heads for a huddled group of people at the far end the settlement, all dressed in black.

WHOOMPH! BOOM! CRACK!

I whip around to see two shockwaves and a trail of jagged crystals speeding toward me.

"This is a *horrible* idea!" I scream, thrusting myself to my feet. By now, my ankle is beginning to go numb, but I take advantage of the adrenaline to chase after the Transporter.

Glancing anxiously over my shoulder, I fling a veil of diamonds behind me, creating a wall to block the oncoming force.

Bursting out from the columns, I find a gathering of muscular Transporters, all looking toward their impromptu leader.

"The metal gives them power!" the Transporter calls to his comrades. "The first chance you get, tear it off of their filthy Scatter bodies!"

Looking nervously over my shoulder, I see my pursuers stomping through the columns, their eyes hungry for destruction.

With metal cuffs glistening, Saunders and Katherine slam their fists into the earth while Perry stomps his booted feet, sending a triple threat of attacks rushing toward me.

Inhaling deeply, I close my eyes and try to control my wild panic. I focus all the heat I have in my body into my hands, channeling all my power into this strange new gift.

Soon, my arms feel like lightning rods, and I aim them at the three Scatters. I release a hysterical cry as a cascade of giant sparkling bullets shooting out at them, neutralizing the shockwaves and crushing the black diamonds to dust.

They wheel backward in shock, but they don't pause for long. All three Scatters touch the metal on their bodies, preparing to unleash their fury on me with full force.

Weak and injured, I know I can't face all three of them alone. I've never used my creation for battle like this, and I don't know how much longer I can keep it up.

My energy spent, I decide to take a risk that could mean my death.

I drop my defenses and step toward them with upturned palms.

"Please, stop!" I cry. "Why are you doing this?"

They recoil at the question—insulted.

"Why?" Katherine snarls. "*Why?* It's because of you that we're here in the first place!" She points a gnarled finger at me.

"How is it *my* fault?" I shout back furiously.

"Because you created us!" Perry roars. "Your very birth ensured that we'd be the rejects of humanity forever!"

"You're wrong, Scatter! Even if I could create people, I'd never create monsters like you!"

The oldest Scatter laughs scathingly. "Foolish boy. You think we were born this way? That Neptuan trick about predicting Scatter traits in children is bullshit. They just wanted to weed out the troublesome kids from the obedient ones. I refused to send one of our youngest to the Scatter settlement, and my captain threw me into this hellhole to rot!"

My jaw drops. Perry used to be a Transporter? How could someone who had dedicated his life to ridding humanity of Scatters become one himself?

"I bet you're a good boy, aren't you?" he continues, smirking. "Listening to your teachers, playing nice with your friends, always keeping the metro's well-being your top priority. You're everything that's wrong with humanity, Creator. With you as a model, anyone who is less than perfect is deemed a Scatter!"

Katherine looks to her fellow Scatter in agreeance. "When the Terra-Marans sent my baby away, I went mad with grief. They made excuses for me for a little while, but when I didn't show signs of getting better, they sent me here myself. Now my baby is dead, and I have no reason to live—except to see you pay, *Creator.* You and all your damn Builders are to blame for my baby's death!"

The bitterness in my heart fractures, and I feel a small wave of sympathy. I'd seen the Transporters take many children away from their families. I'd witnessed their cruelty with my own eyes when they stole my friends from me. In time, most people accepted that it was for the best, but I never did. Until today, I'd always been on Katherine's side.

Now it's Saunders' turn. He looks ruefully at me through puss-filled eyes. "I kept to myself in Terra-Mar, but the Builders didn't like that. They wanted me to be more social, more personable—they wanted me to be something I wasn't. So they sent me here, to a place where I could be as withdrawn as I wanted. Well, I got withdrawn, alright—I spent my days thinking about getting the chance to destroy the person they compared me to: the great and glorious *Creator!*"

I hesitate, wondering if the Scatters were really just misunderstood after all. But then, the memory of my parents in the ditch returns, and so does my conviction for revenge.

I don't care about these freaks' sob stories. That will never be enough to justify murdering innocent people. Perry, Saunders, and Katherine killed the Builders. They killed my mother and father!

Determination growing within me, I dart toward Saunders, crossing one arm over my chest to form a sleek diamond shield that expands up past my head. The Scatters hurriedly slam their fists into the ground, sending shockwaves and black diamonds charging toward me, but I deflect them quickly with a shower of clear diamond bullets.

Before Saunders can attack again, I slam the shield into his face, knocking out several of his teeth. As he falls onto his back, I fling myself onto him and press the shield down on his chest, stifling his wild thrashing. Behind me, the Transporters charge forward and batter the two injured Scatters while they're distracted, viciously tearing the metal off of them.

Saunders snarls through the shield, snapping at me with bloodied gums. I try to reach the cuffs on his wrists, but I can't take them off while still keeping him pressed to the ground. He pounds his fists manically, sending a torrent of shockwaves spinning around us. Out of the corner of my eye, I see the brown-skinned Transporter dart into view just as a rippling shockwave escapes the Scatter's palm. It flies straight at the Transporter's head, knocking him lifelessly to the ground.

"No!" I scream, gaping at the brave man whose name I never knew.

I can't let this happen anymore. I can't let innocent Builders die at the hands of these awful creatures.

Crying at the top of my lungs, I kick myself rightward and tear the glistening metal off of Saunders' wrist. He shrieks with fury, but I jump back on top of him and press all of my weight down so he can't move. Pinning his other wrist with my good foot, I force the metal plate off and fling it over my head.

"*Gaaahhh!*" the Scatter cries. "*Gaaahhh! Gaaahhh! Gaaahhh!*"

I manage to wedge his helmet off too before Saunders flips the shield over in a burst of outrage, sending me sliding face-down across the dirt while he scrambles away.

Rolling onto my back, I raise my arms in front of me, the spear-like tips of two diamond points protruding from my palms. I close one eye to aim at Saunders' fleeing form, preparing to impale him,

I will kill you, Scatter, I think wrathfully, revenge pulsing through my veins. *I will kill you just like you killed those innocent Builders.*

But before I can deliver my shot, a flash of fiery-red leaps out from the forest of columns, tackling the lanky Scatter to the ground. Closing her hands around Saunders's neck, Belinda holds the Scatter down while Chad lands punch after punch into his face, painting his knuckles with the Scatter's blood. When he's incapacitated, Belinda crawls toward the Scatter's feet and tears the glistening metal off of his ankles.

I inhale a breath of relief, but just as I do, a sharp pain streaks down my cheek. I lift my hands instinctively to the source of pain and bring them away stained with blood.

That's when I notice the thin iron spear sticking out of the ground next to me, mere centimeters away. It must have grazed my cheek when it landed, but that's surely not what it was meant to do. Gazing up at the black diamond infrastructure, I see a slender girl standing on the middle-most platform. She wears a navy Terra-Maran sweater and charcoal-gray pants that are many sizes too small, and her blonde ponytail is streaked with dirt. If it weren't for the years of undernourishment in the Scatter settlement, her sunken cheeks would be much fuller.

"Joy!" I cry in disbelief.

I thought I'd never see her again.

In a flash, the girl I used to know disappears into the shadows.

Where is she going?

I slap my burning hands to the soft dirt, imagining a platform growing up under me, sending me closer up toward my friend. Soon, the Scatters and Builders fall away beneath me.

Reaching my destination, I find the girl lurking a distance away from me, her palms aimed at my face.

"Joy!" I call again, limping onto the sleek platform. One hand still rests on my wounded cheek. "It's me, Joy! It's Alan. Don't you remember me?"

Her brows narrow contemptuously, and with one metal-clad hand, she sends a bouquet of iron spears shooting toward me.

Yelping in surprise, I dive out of the way and fall painfully onto the icy floor. Joy's metal armor glows in the dimness as she raises her arms up at the ceiling, opening some sort of portal above her. Bending her knees, she leaps gracefully through it, vanishing from sight.

"Wait, Joy!" I shout, scrambling up to my feet. I manage to limp under the portal before it closes, peering up through it to see her small body bounding swiftly through more portals open within the higher levels.

What are you doing, Alan? I think. I have no idea where I'm about to send myself, but I hold my breath and jump as high as I can, launching my body into the portal after my friend.

"Wait, Joy, stop!" I call fervently as the levels rush past me. Her figure flashes in and out of sight with each new portal we pass through. Around me, I catch glimpses of the quickly changing surroundings—the twisting bridges and staircases growing more intricate with the ever increasing altitude.

Finally, Joy stops at one of the levels above me and dashes out of sight.

I leap awkwardly out of the portal on what I think is the right level and stumble to a stop, trying to get my bearings. I find her standing a distance away at the bottom of a twisting ramp. Next to her is a boy a few inches taller than her, with long blonde hair cut unevenly above his shoulders. His body is longer and thinner now, but his face is just like I remember from four years ago.

"Sal!"

They're still alive! My friends are still alive!

Gesturing wildly, I cry, "It's me, Sal! It's Alan!"

But just like Joy, Sal has no happiness to greet me with. The two of them exchange a knowing look and reach over their shoulders to grab the spears that are strapped to their backs. To my horror, they crouch and prepare to strike.

Why are they doing this? I wonder desperately. *Why are my friends attacking me?*

On either side of the ramp, Sal and Joy dart toward me, aiming their spears at my belly. I swipe my arms up when they get close enough, knocking the weapons out of their hands with a sheet of diamond shards, but it doesn't deter them for long. In a moment, the metal on their bodies begins to glow in preparation for another attack.

"Joy, Sal, why won't you talk to me?" I plead, dropping my defenses.

Sal holds his arm out and conjures another spear, seemingly out of thin air. "What's there to talk about? You abandoned us four years ago when Ruben gave us to the Transporters."

He releases the spear with a forceful wave of his arm and I bring up yet another shield to block it. With a *clang*, it clatters back down to the platform.

"I never abandoned you!" I scream from behind the shield. "I went after you, but there were too many people in the way. I couldn't get to you fast enough!"

"Come on, Alan. You could've created your own way up to us," Joy snaps. "How hard would it have been for you to *imagine* yourself another elevator?"

My breath catches in my throat. "I... I didn't think of that at the time. I was panicking!"

"Oh, please," Joy scoffs. "You really expect us to believe that? Level-headed Alan lost his cool? You didn't care about us. And you definitely didn't need us. Not after you made your little time machine."

Sal cringes. "That's why you were Ruben's favorite. The *Creator* could do anything. He didn't need any help. Why should he care if his friends turned out to be Scatters? He had a time machine. He was going to save the world."

"I *was* going to save the world!" I bellow. "I was about to go back and undo all of this, but Ruben made me stay."

Before the enraged boy can throw another spear at me, I leap forward and punch him straight in the jaw, sending him tumbling backward onto the floor. I straighten to see a cloud of sharpened bolts soaring at me from Joy's direction, and I throw my arms to deflect them with a crystal shield.

"You listened to *everything* Ruben said!" the girl yells. "Did you never once think that he was using you for his own whims?"

"Of course I did!" I growl back. "But creating the time machine was going to help all of humanity! It was going to help us prosper in the colonies, like they were never destroyed!"

"Stop making excuses, Alan!" she shrieks, her cheeks flushing with fury. "You never thought for yourself. You might be the Creator, but you were always Ruben's pawn. You didn't even stop him when he started sending away innocent Builders."

"I tried! But he convinced me that you were just becoming what you already were!"

"SHUT UP, SHUT UP, SHUT UP!" Sal screams.

From behind, he locks his icy fingers around my neck, pulling me backward onto the floor. My head hits the surface so hard that I nearly lose consciousness. Feeling my breath leak out of my lungs, I try to pry Sal's fingers off, but he's too strong.

"You're the biggest hypocrite!" he shouts, his teeth bared in pure loathing. "I want to *feel* you die!"

Out of the corner of my eye, I see Joy produce another round of bolts, her armor glowing with the effort. But just as the girl launches the metal at me, I summon what's left of my strength and kick Sal in her direction.

Shock washes over his face as the bolts penetrate his back, their tips so long and pointed that they protrude out of his chest. His grip loosens from my neck, and his arms slump onto the platform.

"Sal!" Joy yelps, dashing forward.

Gasping for air, I crawl back from the boy, his woody-brown eyes still trained on me as he loses consciousness. Behind him, Joy kneels, whimpering. Her trembling hands scan his limp body hopelessly.

So this is what it feels like to be a Scatter, I think. *This is what it feels like to take life.*

The hairs on my neck begin to prickle as an eerie coldness presses against my skin, sucking the heat out of my body.

Turning around, I see a boy's emaciated figure standing motionless a few feet away, half of his body shrouded in shadow. His skin is a shade paler than olive, and his hair hangs sloppily into his forest-green eyes, which look fiercely at me.

Unlike the others, there's not a hint of metal on his body.

"Garrett..."

CHAPTER 16

When I saw Joy and Sal, I knew that he'd be here. I've wanted him with me all these years, and now, I'm finally seeing him again.

Suddenly, all the guilt I felt on the day he was sent away tumbles back—all the terror of watching the Transporters' shock batons beat against his small, thirteen-year-old body.

I'm sorry! I'd wept to him through the hatch. *I'm sorry I couldn't protect you.*

But anger soon replaces my guilt as the sight of my dead parents flashes behind my eyes.

How could you kill my parents?! I think furiously at him. *You were my best friend. How could you do that to me?*

With an unwavering gaze, Garrett raises his hands calmly and pushes his palms forward, sending a rush of icy-blue wind rolling in my direction.

Throwing up my own arms in defense, I send a burst of hot orange flames roiling out against it. The two collide in a brilliant eruption of frost and heat, but the flames don't stand a chance. They wink out in an instant and the cold washes over me like the freezing ocean water outside.

What is this? I think in alarm, feeling my body temperature drop drastically. It's like my very lifeblood is freezing in my veins, zapping all the heat inside me. Looking down, I find a thin sheet of ice coating my body.

Without a word, Garrett turns around and runs up a ramp that hadn't been there moments ago, dashing up to the top level after it settles at his feet.

"Wait, Garrett!" I call, holding one arm out to him. I have so many questions.

I twist against the suit of ice that covers me, sending tiny shards flinging across the platform. Slapping my palms against the floor, I feel a welcome rush of heat as the clear platform I'd used to chase Joy returns beneath me, growing at a slant as it elevates me up over the ramp after Garrett.

Joy screams in outrage as I escape, tossing spears wildly, but her rage inhibits her accuracy and I duck out of their way.

"You'll pay for this!" she shouts after me, but I'm already out of range.

The bright fluorescent lights burn down on me as I approach the highest level. Halting at the top of the ramp, I find Garrett standing with his back to me near the far edge of the platform.

My ankle feels like a foreign object now from all the damage I've done to it, and I stumble off the platform awkwardly.

"Garrett," I call to him angrily. "I'm not this evil person you all are making me out to be. Don't you remember when we played catch in Terra-Mar? We were friends. *Best* friends. You know me. You know I didn't do this to you."

He seems to growl at my words, but doesn't turn. Tiny tendrils of ice snake out across the platform from his feet.

"Garrett, *talk to me!*" I plead. "Why did you bring all the Builders here? Why did you bring *me* here?"

Finally, he turns, and to my horror I see that he'd been forming an orb between his hands the whole time—it's black and bottomless, like a vacuum.

"You were never supposed to come here," he says with a slow shake of his head. For a moment I think he's talking about the Scatter settlement, but then he goes on, "The Creator has no place in this world. You should've never been born."

I watch in frozen shock as the black orb leaves his hand and sails toward me, growing like an enormous mouth coming to swallow me within its jaws. It swells so large that my only option to escape it is to jump off the edge of the platform...and fall to my death.

My instincts tell me to close my eyes, but I resist. I keep them wide open. I want to look my best friend in the eye—the boy who I cared for and trusted so much—as he ends my life.

"I'm so sorry," I utter under my breath as the orb grows ever closer.

This never would've happened if I'd just been able to protect him.

Suddenly, five small figures dash out from behind Garrett, each with a collection of glowing metal in their hands. I watch in confusion as they gather in front of me—Shawn, Lawrence, Cal, Owen, and Beckett joining shoulder-to-shoulder to form a protective wall.

"No, boys, stop!" I cry, reaching out to push them away.

But it's too late. The orb is upon us.

Before it can make contact, the boys thrust the glistening metal pieces forward—helmets, wristlets, and anklets. When they collide, the orb bounces sharply back toward its maker.

His sharp green eyes bulging in astonishment, Garrett swipes his hand out quickly, shielding himself behind a thick slab of black diamond that emerges from the floor. When the orb makes contact with the sleek surface, it hits with a loud *CRACK* and dissipates into oblivion, sending shards of destruction slamming into the boy.

Garrett stumbles backward, shrieking in pain when his left foot twists into an awkward position. He lands on the floor with a sickly *THUD.*

The five boys in front of me slump down onto their knees, panting as if they've been running for hours.

"What the hell were you thinking doing something crazy like that?!" I holler at them. "And how did you get all the way up here?"

"Um, we *climbed,*" Shawn says, pointing over my shoulder at the ramp.

Lawrence nods. "How else were we supposed to help you?"

Behind them, Garrett releases an agonized cry as he struggles to his feet. After glancing briefly down at his ankle, he raises his eyes chillingly to me with the same look of rage from that day in the docking pod.

Without speaking, he turns to the far end of the level, limping violently, clutching his left leg.

My heart pounding at top speed, I throw myself up and round past the boys, struggling to walk myself.

"Wait, what're you doing, Alan?!" Beckett calls after me.

"Don't go after the Scatter!"

But I ignore them. I need answers.

Seeing the edge loom closer, I hesitate, hoping that Garrett will slow too.

He doesn't. Instead, he thrusts his hands forward and sends a black diamond bridge cascading from the edge. It lodges into the enclosure, where an iron hatch forms in the glass. From the darkness outside, the glittering enigma materializes in the light of the settlement.

So it was the Scatters after all, I think, my already infuriated thoughts spiraling out of control. With Garrett as their captain, the Scatters destroyed Neptua and Terra-Mar, then came back to kill anyone who got away. It was the Scatters all along.

It was *Garrett* all along.

"Stop, Garrett!" I roar, thrusting my hands out to form a clear diamond barrier in front of him, stopping him halfway to his escape vessel.

He whips around and looks vengefully at me, his shoulders rising and falling as he pants.

"You know what civilization really needs, Alan?" he shouts. "Not a damn time machine, but some *compassion!* Even if we were able to go back in time to the Mars colony, we wouldn't have saved humanity. Wars would still have been fought, and destruction would still have prevailed because of people like you, who believe you're better than everyone else. Why do you think the Earth Purists struck back? Because they were persecuted for being what they were! Just like the Scatters who were sent to die in this settlement."

He points a rigid finger to the ground below. "Look at the Builders down there. They always preached that they were incapable of destruction—that their purpose was to build great things. But look at what they did to the Scatters! They destroyed our lives! Look down there and tell me that they didn't *completely destroy our lives!*"

Hesitantly, I turn back to the settlement and gaze down at the three Scatters on the ground level. The Transporters around Perry are relentless, punching him until blood oozes out of his every orifice. Katherine wails with each blow of the Transporters' fists to her side, crying out for the baby that was taken from her. Saunders spits up blood as Belinda and Chad plant kick after kick into his belly.

Builders don't destroy, Gina's words echo in my ears.

But look at what they're doing now, I think, my eyes still locked on the heinous scene below. Is it any better than what the Scatters did?

"You're all hypocrites!" Garrett barks.

And he's right. The Builders are hypocrites. The Scatters down there wouldn't be what they are if it weren't for the Builders. The Builders created the Scatters.

And if it weren't for *me,* there wouldn't be any Builders to begin with.

Finally I realize why the Scatters are so angry with me. Until I started creating, the Terra-Marans were all just people.

What have I done?

"The Builders down there lost their minds in this settlement after only three days," Garrett explains gravely. "The Scatters have been here for *years*, and they're still alive. We are *stronger* than the Builders! We are *better* than them! We don't need their food, their clothes, or their inventions. We don't need *anything* from them!"

I turn back to my friend, meeting his piercing glare.

"You're not the only one who's extraordinary, Alan," he spits. "I might not have been Ruben's golden child, but I am stronger than you. Always have been."

At his words, the memories of Garrett's acts of strength race through my mind—the dent in the enclosure, the crumbled sheet of steel in the lab, the broken time machine—all things that a young boy could not possibly have done with physical strength alone.

How did I not see it before?

Garrett's not a Builder, or a Scatter, or even a Neutral.

He's the Destroyer, and I'm the Creator.

He's the lethal left hand, and I'm the regal right.

He's the cold of dark, and I'm the warmth of light.

We are perfect opposites.

We are *each other's* opposite.

Suddenly, I no longer have to wonder what happened to him after he was sent away from Terra-Mar. Out of sight from the Builders, he spent four years developing his own abilities, waiting for the perfect opportunity to strike back. One by one he took the Transporters' shock batons and transformed them into the metal armor that adorned his fellow Scatters. Through it, he must have been able to project his abilities to his comrades, something I never even tried to do. That's how the Scatters created the holes in Terra-Mar's enclosure, and how they sealed up the one here just a few minutes earlier.

That's his ability: to destroy, and also to recreate. To make something whole out of what's broken. To glorify again what was previously marred.

It *is* better than simply creating something for the first time.

Garrett is better than me in every way.

Turning back to the barrier that I created, the Destroyer swipes his hand in front of him, sending the same black orb spinning from his palms to disintegrate the diamond wall. As he proceeds to the hatch, a thick column of black diamond shoots up on his right and out steps Joy,

Sal's limp body draped across her shoulders. A second column emerges on the other side of the bridge, where the disheveled Saunders and Perry carry a broken Katherine between them, her bony feet dragging beneath her.

With a *CLONK*, the glittering submarine outside locks onto the hatch and the bridge whirrs as it drains of water. His steely-green eyes flooded with hatred, Garrett turns back to me once more and says, "There's no place for us in a world of filthy hypocrites. I'm taking these broken people to a place of their own, where I can help them rebuild their lives, their minds, and their spirits."

But all I can think as I watch Joy yank open the hatch is why Garrett didn't take me along with the rest of the Terra-Marans. I was asleep in my pod the whole time. If he truly thought I was a hypocrite and wanted me to die, why didn't he just destroy me along with the enclosure?

I still have so many questions.

As if reading my mind, the Destroyer growls back at me, "*Never* try to find me again, Alan. You and the Builders are *not welcome* where we're going."

My vision blurs with tears. "You don't have to go, Garrett, please! We can figure this out together. I can help the Builders understand!"

"They'll never understand," Garrett says somberly, already halfway into the hatch. "Builders don't like destruction because they can't see the beautiful recovery after it—how things can become stronger, *better*, after all is lost and gone. I'm going to create my own settlement, where the Scatters can recover what little bit of humanity they've salvaged through their exile here in this heartless place."

And with that, he disappears into the bridge, swinging the door shut behind him.

No, I think, shaking my head. *NO!*

He can't just leave me with these half-answered questions. He *can't*.

I collide against the hatch just as the wheel lurches rightward, locking with a finite *CLANK*. The iron melts into transparency and fades back into the glass, through which I can see Garrett walking into the enigma's illuminated entry area ahead.

"You can't go, Garrett!" I scream, pounding against the glass. "I won't let you go until you answer my questions!"

Whether he can somehow hear me or just notices me flailing behind the glass, the boy halts in the entryway and turns to face me, his expression terrifyingly dark.

For a moment, the two of us regard each other, not as Builder and Scatter, nor Creator and Destroyer, but as friends reflecting on the years we've lost—the time that was taken from us.

And that's when I realize, despite all the research and hours we spent trying and failing to create the time machine, it was our friendship that was our greatest creation.

Or was it all just part of my imagination?

"Questions," I mouth to him through the enclosure, my voice escaping in a weak exhale. "I still have questions."

Pursing his cold lips, Garrett turns abruptly back around and vanishes into the ship.

"No, no, *NO!*" I holler, slamming my fist again. Blood from my knuckles smears across the glass, but I don't stop. *"GET BACK HERE, DAMMIT! I NEED ANSWERS!"*

It's just like the day four years ago, when he was taken from Terra-Mar. Only this time, Garrett isn't being sent away. He's leaving on his own accord—leaving me to wallow in a never-ending pool of questions, forever wondering why, why, why...

I strike the glass out of anger for my dead parents—for all the dead Builders and Scatters and Neutrals, and whatever other types of people existed.

And I strike it for myself, because I don't know where I fit in to all this. I don't know where I'm supposed to go now, or what I'm supposed to do. I don't know anything anymore.

Below me, the Builders cheer for their victory against the Scatters. After all, it is always the hypocrites who prevail.

I never thought that my creations could cause so much destruction, so much pain and suffering. I always thought that I was great, that what I did made people happy and bettered humanity's future. How could so much goodness bring so many calamities? How could the light that I thought was chasing away the darkness cast even more darkness?

Was it really Garrett who lured me to this place, to discover how wrong I'd been?

Or was it me all along, finally realizing the inevitable?

CHAPTER 17

My body slides weakly to the floor, my bloody hands leaving streaks as I go. I stare out at the endless darkness, as if by waiting long enough I'll convince Garrett to come back.

He never does.

I don't know how long I kneel there before someone's hand eventually lands on my shoulder. I turn around to see Ruben peering sympathetically down at me through his cracked glasses.

"I suspected there was something off about him the minute he scattered those blocks when you were kids," he says gravely. "And that dent in the enclosure confirmed it. I included him in the time machine project because I wanted to be sure of what he was before I sent him away. We hadn't seen a Scatter in so long… I couldn't be certain until he destroyed the time machine. At that point, I wanted to keep him as far away from you as possible. I wanted to *protect* you from him. If Terra-Mar lost its Creator, there would be nothing to keep the balance of our civilization."

I peer silently behind him at the other Builders who now assemble on the ramp in a big crowd. They're exhausted, starved, and disheveled, but there's lots of them. Scanning their numbers, I realize that there are many more survivors than I thought—enough to start a new settlement.

Rising to my feet, I limp toward the Builders, their ashen faces looking expectantly back at me.

A burly Transporter with bristly black hair steps forward. "Keegan was one of our best," he says lowly. "He was a great believer in you, Creator."

I pause, not recognizing the name, but then I nod solemnly. He must be talking about the brown-skinned Transporter who perished at Saunders's hand.

"Keegan's martyrdom will not be forgotten," I reply.

Chad steps out of the pack, rubbing his sore knuckles. "Both Terra-Mar and Neptua are destroyed now," he says worriedly. "Where will we live?"

I draw in a sharp breath.

Of course. That must be what all of them are worried about.

He wants me to create a new settlement for the Builders.

Limping to the edge of the platform, I look down at the ground level far below me. It's littered with bodies and dented with craters, but the foundation remains intact. This isn't the home the Builders want, but it's the only one left.

And I can rebuild it.

I spread my arms wide, shaking with soreness and fatigue. The familiar warming sensation takes a moment to emerge after so much effort already expended, but eventually it comes, surging through my body.

From out of the dirt rises a grid of colossal iron beams reaching up to each level below me. They flatten and merge into six bridges, extending out toward the edges of the enclosure and lodging into the glass. Clusters of pods bubble up at the ends of each bridge to form the six locales of the new Terra-Mar, and within each pod materialize all the same appliances and furnishings that the Builders are used to.

Upon each of the black diamond platforms beneath me, I create the workings of classrooms, including everything from the desks the Builders will sit in to the tablet computers they'll use to store their data. I can't reinvent the files from the past—that history will have to remain in the past—but I can give the Builders everything they need to create a new future.

At the base of the enclosure, I form five titanium submarines that are identical to The Liberation, each with their bridges docked at the enclosure's hatches.

Turning around, I aim my palms at the shattered fluorescent lights and imagine a set of replacements. Soon, new bulbs emerge, alighting with freshly restored electricity from the hydro turbines on the mountainside that churn creakily to life.

The new settlement created, I drop my arms and wobble around to face the Builders, who have spread out toward the edges of the platform to gaze at the wonders around them.

Ruben smiles contentedly at me, just like he always does. He pulls me into a firm embrace and I hold my breath as he squeezes. After a moment, he steps back, still grasping me by my shoulders. "Now that the Scatters are all gone, we can finally live in a civilization without destruction. More importantly, we can continue with our experiments on creating life!"

His thin lips curl into an excited grin, the ambitious flame returning to his copper-brown eyes, but when I shake my head, his expression falters.

"As long as the Builders exist, there will always be Scatters," I tell him. "If not now, then in the future."

My teacher is aghast, and rightfully so. I've never spoken out against him like this.

I continue, "The only way to eradicate this divide is through compassion. It's only when we can learn to care for each other despite our differences that there will be no more conflict, no more war, no more destruction."

I walk past Ruben toward a clearing at the center of the level. Lifting my arms in front of me again, I summon the familiar warming sensation and imagine a tower of neatly stacked tools—hammers, nails, wrenches, screwdrivers—glinting like brilliant silver fish under the fluorescent lights. In a moment, they wink to life, and I hear the people around me murmur with wonder.

"Look at all that I've created for you," I say to them. "This is everything the Builders will ever need to maintain this new settlement. On the ground, there are seeds and roots that can be cultivated into food. You can use the desalinaters in the pods to water them, and the lights above will continue to shine for as long as the ocean exists. Outside, there are submarines for you to harvest fish. You don't need me to create anything for you anymore—you have everything you need to keep this new settlement flourishing."

From the corner of my eye I see Belinda's fiery hair, and I limp over to her, shuffling the shards around my feet. Her crystal-blue eyes look quizzically back at me as I pull her into a gentle embrace.

"I love you, sister," I tell her, then plant a light kiss on her cheek. "Take care of everyone. Never let anyone change who you are."

Chad stands to her right, and I turn to him next.

"Thank you, brother," I tell him, taking his hand firmly. "Be strong, and protect your home. Remember that all human lives are necessary, both Builder and Scatter."

Then I turn to the five boys standing together at the center of the level behind me, their eyes gazing wide and innocently up at me.

Trudging over to them, I brush the broken glass away and rest one knee on the floor, smiling wearily at each boy in turn. Three days ago, I couldn't wait to find the lost Builders, just so I could get these kids out of my hair. Now, I grow nervous thinking of the lonely trip ahead of me.

"You're all friends," I tell them. "Here, in this brave new settlement, you're going to learn and build together. Sometimes you'll agree, and other times, you won't. Those disagreements may lead you to fight. When this happens, remember your friendship—it's what will keep you together, even when others try to divide you."

I hold back tears after the last sentence leaves my lips. I wish someone could have said that to me and Garrett. Creation and Destruction are both necessary, but we never got a chance to understand what we were before we got ripped away from each other.

As I rise back up to my feet, my hand brushes past a swell on my pant leg, and I peer down at it. Reaching into my pocket, my fingers close around a curved leathery object—it's my baseball.

My first creation. I can't believe it's been with me this whole time.

Ruben still stands near the glass, looking absolutely distraught. I beckon to him, holding the baseball out in front of me, and his eyes drift wonderingly to it. When he reaches me, I set it in his upturned palms.

Ruben's lesson was what prompted my first creation. It's only fitting that he become its keeper. I don't think I'll be playing much catch where I'm going, anyway.

"Are you sure?" he asks, though whether he's questioning my gift or my decision to leave, I'm not sure.

I nod once, then turn again and limp back to the platform's edge.

"You're the *only* Creator we have," he calls, his voice quivering. "We still need you to continue the legacy of the Builders. Please, don't leave us."

I stop, staring dead ahead into the endless abyss outside.

There are so many things I could tell him right now. Like that he was the one to blame for the wrath of the Destroyer—that he provoked Garrett to do what he did. It was Ruben's misguided judgment and prejudice that caused all this to happen—for so many kind people to be sent to the Scatter settlement, for the loss of so many Builders' lives, even for the ultimate destruction of Neptua and Terra-Mar.

But none of that matters anymore. Now that I've given them everything they need, none of that matters at all.

I turn back around to find Ruben only steps away, one hand still cupped around the baseball. I take his free hand and lay mine over his, then lift it a few seconds later, leaving a shiny new pair of glasses behind.

This is my last creation for him. From now on, he will just have to build the things he needs himself.

Without another word, I hobble to the edge, feeling the eyes of every Builder following me pleadingly. Holding my hands out, I imagine a wide column of gleaming diamond rising up from the ground, past the bridges and platforms of the new locales. When I look down, it's there at my feet, a narrow slide extending down to the ground below me.

I crouch and push off before any more Builders can protest. As I gain speed, the chill of the rushing air awakens my senses and relieves my aching body. The new settlement rushes past me as I slide—bridges, locales, and classrooms swooping by in a blur.

The slide levels out at the bottom so I can slow to a stop, and I stumble up to my feet, the loose ground feeling strange and uneven under my shoes. I keep my eyes locked on the three hatches in front of me as I walk past the crater, not wanting to see the bodies piled inside. If I have to look at my parents' cold, lifeless forms again, I fear I will completely break down.

Before long I arrive at the centermost hatch. Clasping its wheel, I turn and yank it open, revealing the cold dark path inside.

In a moment's hesitation, I peer back up at the Builders somewhere high above me. I can barely see them past the dizzying twists and turns of the infrastructure's ramps and stairs. Can Belinda still feel my lips on her cheek? Can Chad still feel my grip in his hand? Can the boys still hear my words echoing through their ears?

Is Ruben still hoping that I won't leave?

Those people... they're the *only* people I've ever known. Where I'm going is a mystery, a barren wasteland of questions and uncertainties.

But in my heart I know the choice is already made.

Turning back around, I step somberly inside the bridge and lock the hatch behind me. I limp my way to the vessel's entrance, my shoes making quiet *pangs* as I venture into the void. The bridge momentarily floods with light as I unlock the hatch to the submarine—I can no longer see any of the Builders in the enclosure, but I don't attempt to look for them.

I'm on my own now.

Stepping inside the familiar entry area, I turn to close the hatch, sighing as I tighten the wheel until it locks. After an agonizing climb up the ladder, I hoist myself onto my good foot in the control room and lean against the main panel, scanning my surroundings.

Everything looks exactly like The Liberation—the large window at the front, the control panel with its two levers beneath the sonar screen, even the wall of glowing buttons and gauges. Everything is here except for five loud, annoying, endearing little boys.

Hobbling over to the glowing buttons, I detach the bridge from the settlement with a loud *CLONK*, then turn my attention to the sonar screen nearby. I lift my hand to press the button beneath it, then stop myself.

What are you looking for, Alan? I ask myself, my finger hovering in mid-air. *The only person out here that I want to see doesn't want you to search for him. There's no point in looking for anyone anymore, because no one's looking for you.*

There's nothing in my way now.

I can go wherever I want.

Taking a deep breath, I lay my hands on the levers, urging the engine to life. The ship hums as the propellers begin to spin, easing the submarine off the ocean floor.

For the first time since entering the submarine, I look out through the left window, seeing the glowing settlement falling away.

A strange sinking feeling washes over me.

I thought that freedom would be exhilarating, thrilling, full of promise—but all I feel now is loss.

I have to give up everything I know to move forward.

Looking at the deep dark ocean, all I can think of is the surface... the great, mysterious surface. That's where I wanted to go, and that's where I'm going now.

And so I rise, out of the dark, up from the bottom of the ocean. I'm going somewhere above where there are no Builders, no Scatters, no Neutrals, no settlements.

I'm going above, where there is only freedom.

PART 3

CHAPTER 18

The water brightens from deep azure, to aqua, to baby blue as I approach the surface. For the first time in my life, I see streaks of golden sunlight ripple silkily in the current, and my pulse races with excitement. A breathtaking array of colorful marine life frolics past the front window in vibrant flashes of yellow, orange, and silver. I've never seen colors so bright and alive.

The submarine bursts out of the water with a noisy splash, and as the pressure gauges fall to zero, the engine silences.

After a few deep breaths, I look up at the ceiling—that familiar expanse of metal under which I've grown so weary these past harrowing days. Raising my arms, an impatient streak of heat shoots through me as I build myself a tower to the surface. With a groan of metal, the ceiling dents upward and a ladder drops down with a heavy *CLUNK.*

This is it, I think, panting with anticipating. *I'm finally at the surface, where no Builder or Scatter has ever gone before. This is my final destination.*

Gripping the sides of the ladder, I hop gingerly up the rungs, my swollen ankle protesting the whole way. But even through the pain I smile, because I know that seeing the blue sky will be worth everything I've endured.

Reaching the top of the tower, I feel for the wheel beneath the rounded hatch overhead and heave it open with a loud *CLANG.* My heart threatens to burst as a crisp rush of air—*real* air, not the stale ventilated air from Terra-Mar—blusters through the tower, bringing with it the salty fragrance of the sea. I can hear the sloshing of the waves against the hull.

My hands shake as I pull myself the final distance up the ladder and gaze upward, expecting to see a sprawling expanse of pure blue.

Instead, I find a dull blanket of brown stretching across the sky as far as I can see.

"Huh?" I utter in confusion.

Is this really the surface?

I blink hard a few times, as if my eyes will suddenly show me something different, but of course the next time I open them I find the same endless blanket of light brown murk.

"That can't be the sky..." I groan. "It's not *blue*."

Three large gray creatures soar by overhead, and I dive hurriedly back into the tower, fearing danger. When nothing happens, I crawl tentatively back out again, watching a trio of what I can only guess are seagulls disappear into the distance, clucking gutturally to one another. Taking a deep, calming breath, I turn my eyes to the sky again, still flabbergasted by its appearance.

What's happened to the ozone while the Builders have isolated themselves at the bottom of the sea? The oxygen here is certainly breathable, and the gravity doesn't feel much different from the simulator back in Terra-Mar. Something radical must have changed since my ancestors returned to this planet, but what?

Crestfallen, I turn to the infinite ocean in front of me, where sunlit waves lap carelessly against the submarine.

The Builders were right about one thing, I think wryly. *There's nothing up here—no land, no people. The surface is just a barren stretch of water.*

Exhausted, I lean against the rim of the hatch to take pressure off my ankle. For a few minutes, I close my eyes and indulge in the rolling wind, which cools my sweaty brow.

Now that I've finally emerged from the sea, I suddenly don't feel such a raging aversion to it. There might not be anything up here on the surface, but I feel completely at peace, like everything that's happened to me was all for this one glorious, blissful moment.

This is where I've wanted to be my whole life, and I feel like I could stay here forever. Or at least for about five minutes, until I realize all the things I'm missing.

"Hey, there!" a gruff voice calls from behind me.

Jumping in surprise, I spin around to face the stern, knocking my ribs painfully against the tower in the process. To my shock, I see a man standing on a sandy beach only a few meters away. He's a tall, tanned figure draped in some sort of animal hide, and a bushy beard grows down from his chin. Beside him sit two women—one older, perhaps mid-forties, and the other around my age. They share the same complexion as the man, the younger one clutching a loose bundle in her arms.

The man waves one long arm at me. "Hey, there! Hey!"

My jaw drops. I can't believe it. There are *people* here—people standing on *land.*

The Builders were wrong after all.

In a hurry, I clamber clumsily out from the tower and lower myself down to the top of the hull a few feet below me. The exterior of the ship is cold and slick.

The man stops waving abruptly, then turns his palms out in front of him, pushing them repeatedly toward me.

I don't recognize this gesture, and I'm too far to see the expression on his face, but I raise my arms above my head and wave back to him.

"Hello, *hello!*" I call excitedly.

The man continues to push his palms in my direction. Beside him, the two women rise to their feet and dash over to him, seemingly telling him something.

The sub rocks dangerously underneath me, and I wobble on my injured ankle. "Hey! Hello!"

People! There are people here!

I start to take a step further down the stern, but my foot loses purchase on the slippery deck and my legs come out from under me. The world tilts sideways as I tumble into the freezing ocean, my vision blurring between brown sky and blue water. I splash frantically in the water, shouting for help and flailing every limb. Panic rushes through me as I kick my legs frantically, trying desperately to stay above the surface.

That's when I realize that I don't know how to swim.

I've spent years trying to get out of the ocean, but I've never tried to get *through* it.

And now I'm drowning.

Salt water fills my mouth and pours down into my lungs, threatening to drag me under the surface. As I fight to stay afloat, a strange nipping feeling surrounds me, like little clamps clipping away at my skin. Scanning around me, I find the colorful little fish that I adored moments ago now pecking away at my body.

They're eating me! I think in horror, smacking frenetically at them only to be blinded by fistfuls of water. *They're actually eating me alive!*

Somehow I manage to stay above water long enough to see the man on the beach lift his clothes over his head and fetch a wooden spear from the sand. Jogging quickly down to the shore, he dives headfirst into the water.

My body sinks back down beneath the surface, where the fish descend ravenously upon me, pulling me apart one little bite at a time. What air I have left escapes my lungs in a cloud of bubbles and is quickly replaced by an influx of water.

I flail and scream for as long as I can before my consciousness finally starts slipping away. The blur starts at the edges of my vision and quickly shrouds my view until and all I see is darkness.

This is it, I think, feeling as heavy as iron as I drift down beneath. *This is the end for me.*

Then, from somewhere above, I feel a pull on the neck of my sweater, lifting me upward until I emerge back above the surface. There, the gruff voice exclaims, "Hah! You damn finned miscreants!"

Splashing sounds soon follow, but I can't open my eyes. I'm already slipping away...

A few moments later, I feel solid land beneath me, the heaviness of my wet clothes weighing me down.

My back slams against the sand, and I wretch forward, coughing water from my lungs. Flopping back down, my eyes flutter open, squinting up at the burning ball in the sky. Voices surround me, speaking inaudibly.

Then, once again, the darkness claims me. I close my eyes, slipping back into unconsciousness.

....

The sound of crackling fire wakes me. As I ease my eyes open, my blurry vision focuses on the three people I saw before, now sitting with their backs turned to me. Between them I can see four long skewers of roasting fish and a large tent beyond that, the animal hide entrance flapping in the salty sea wind.

Rolling to my side, I press my palm against the leathery mat beneath me and push myself up to a sitting position. The damp sand feels both strange and satisfying as I dig my toes into it. A gentle breeze passes and I shiver slightly, only to look down and find that I'm wearing nothing but my pants. Embarrassed, I search the ground quickly to locate my sweater. To my relief, I find it folded neatly next to my shoes and socks. They all still feel slightly moist when I touch them—I haven't been unconscious for long.

Pulling my sweater back on (which is frayed from all the carnivorous fish), I'm shocked to find that the soreness and ache I'd felt from the day's battle has suddenly vanished. I feel strangely rejuvenated, like I've been sleeping for weeks. Running my hand along my left cheek, I can't find my cut. Then, looking at the backs of my hands, I realize that my knuckles are completely healed. I lift my pant leg to check my swollen ankle, but it's now shrunken back to its normal size.

"How...?"

I straighten my leg and rotate my foot, testing my ankle's resiliency. It feels perfectly fine. There's no pain, whatsoever.

Something healed me completely while I slept.

Hearing my rustling, the now fully-clothed man glances over his shoulder at me, then crosses the distance between us to sit on the mat next to me. He regards me solemnly with a pair of pecan-brown eyes.

"I was telling you to stay where you were," he says. "The fish right off the shore eat human flesh, and you didn't have the proper weapons to fend them off."

My cheeks burn with humiliation. "I thought you were just greeting me."

He smiles. "Well now we know you're good fish bait."

There's a beat of silence as the two of us stare at the darkening sky. In my peripheral vision I see the two women glancing curiously at me, but when I meet their eyes they quickly return their attention to the roasting fish.

"Are you feeling better?" the man asks knowingly.

My eyes widen with eagerness. "Oh, yes. I'm feeling *great,* actually. I sprained my ankle before I came here, but now it feels fine—*better* in fact."

The man nods absentmindedly, returning his gaze to the sky. Ribbons of orange, ochre, and burgundy paint the horizon.

"The sunset," the man indicates. "It's beautiful, isn't it?"

I purse my lips, uncertain. "Actually, I've never seen one of these before, but yes, it *is* beautiful. It's the most beautiful sight I've ever seen."

"*You* are something we've never seen before," the man says. He gestures to my hair. "It's so bright." Then he points to my eyes. "They're *blue*. It's very strange."

Now it's my turn to smile. "Well, I don't think *you're* strange. Where I come from, there are people with all kinds of physical features—yours, mine, and many others."

The man pauses, looking at me blankly. "You came from the ocean," he says, and points over at my submarine still floating a distance off the beach. "From that... boat."

"Actually, it's a submarine," I confirm. "It's a vehicle for underwater transport. It has a titanium alloy hull, pressure gauges, a nuclear engine—"

But his expression goes blank once again. He has no idea what I'm talking about.

I fall silent, and the two of us stare off into the ever dimming sky. A damp wind blows up from the ocean, ruffling our hair.

"What's happened up here?" I ask wonderingly. "All these centuries since our fall from the stars... Where I come from, we believe that the earth is *covered* with water. How is it that you're here, on this land mass? How could land be here *at all?* Are there other people here, too?"

The man's forehead wrinkles. "I do not know why you think the earth has been covered with water, but there are *many* people here. This land stretches very far. There are people who live in forests, swamps, caves, and beneath the shadows of giant mountains. There are those who live in the desert, and in ice and snow. People have lived here for centuries, and thrived even though the earth has changed. People will always live and thrive, no matter what hardships may stand in their way."

I'm speechless. All this time that the Builders have hidden themselves in the ocean, life has been prospering here on the surface. How have we been so ignorant as to not come up and explore this place? All the images in Terra-Mar's database model the earth as a colossal sphere of liquid floating aimlessly in space.

They were afraid, I conclude despondently. *The Builders were afraid that if they were wrong about the surface being barren, they would lose all the amazing settlements and submarines that they'd built down there, at the bottom of the ocean. They didn't want to start all over again.*

They just wanted to bury themselves in the past, in the ruins of what those Earth Purists on the Mars colony created.

I look down at the sand, clumpy with the footprints of the many people who must have certainly roamed here. An overwhelming sense of loss crashes down on me for all the time that we wasted. If we had only set aside our fear—our pride—we could have lived up here, in the wide open space of the surface.

"This place, where you come from," the man asks. "Where is it?"

I look up at him, debating whether or not to tell him about the destroyed metro—about the fleets of nuclear submarines docked outside the sprawling Scatter settlement, ready to rise at a moment's notice. These people have no idea what exists beneath them in the dark depths of the sea, hidden away from sight.

"It's a place far away, beneath the ocean."

The man doesn't press, seemingly sensing my reluctance to elaborate.

After another contemplative pause, he puts his hand over his chest and says, "Jarvis." Then he points to the elderly woman shifting the firewood with a stick. "My partner, Meckel." Finally he gestures to the younger woman beside her, who coos at a baby swaddled in her arms. "My daughter, Edna, and her son. Edna's partner passed some time ago. He was sick, and we could not heal him in time."

"Oh," I utter, and look down at the sand, the last few rays of sunlight disappearing over them. The familiar wave of sympathy washes over me, and I think of how sad the young woman must be, with a baby who will never know his father.

"We catch the man-eating fish, and trade them with the merchants that we meet on our pilgrimages."

When I look back up, I realizing that he's waiting for me to respond. "Oh, uh, Alan," I sputter. "My name is Alan. I'm... just a boy from the ocean." I reach up to my face nervously to check my scar again, and remember that it's gone.

"How did you heal me?" I wonder aloud, pointing at my smoothened cheek. "I had a cut here. Usually my wounds take weeks to heal, and even then, they leave a scar. But now it's like... it's like I'm born again."

The man studies my astonishment, and simply chuckles.

"We healed you using something that is very precious and valuable across this land," he says. "I will show it to you tomorrow. It is somewhat complicated to explain right now."

I begin to respond, but exhaustion suddenly overwhelms me, and I yawn.

"Rest," the man says. "My family and I will bring you some food."

Jarvis rises and returns to the two women in front of the fire, so I lie back down on the mat, watching the three of them rotate the skewered fish. The flicker of the fire is hypnotic, and I watch it until my eyes start to flutter. Before long, I'm drifting back to sleep.

CHAPTER 19

The dawn air still holds the evening chill, and the seagulls above cluck frenziedly for their breakfasts. Only a short distance from the shore, I can feel the salty spray as the waves crash against the rocks. I kneel in a circle with Meckel and Edna as Jarvis retrieves a straw sack from the tent, the contents inside, glowing through. He holds it reverently as he comes to stand between us.

"Rain," he explains, reaching into the sack. "It is a precious gift from Kalono, bestowed to us through the Rain-gatherers of Boreala." Withdrawing a handful of what appear to be luminescent droplets, he approaches his partner and deposits the Rain into her cupped palms.

I stare in fascination—they are the same glowing droplets that I saw in the clearing on my way to the Scatter settlement. I never thought I'd see them again, especially not up here. It's as if something brought them back to me.

Proceeding toward Edna now, Jarvis spills a handful of Rain into her palms too. "We make several pilgrimages every year to Boreala to trade our fish for more Rain. It cannot be melted by heat—only by prayers."

As the man proceeds to me, I copy the two women by cupping my palms in front of me.

"This is what healed you yesterday," he explains. "Rain is one of the last precious treasures left in this world. Entire wars have been fought over it, and lives have been lost. But those who wage war for it can never taste its sweet serenity."

Jarvis withdraws another handful of glowing Rain and deposits it into my palms. But the second the droplets touch my skin, they transform into a cool, radiant liquid that spills through my fingers into the sand.

I look up in confusion, only to find Jarvis and the women staring wide-eyed back at me, shocked. Meckel and Edna still hold their own rations of Rain in solid droplet form.

"You!" Jarvis exclaims, his expression bouncing between disbelief and wonder.

"I-I don't know what happened!" I sputter hastily, holding my wet hands up in surrender. "I swear, I didn't do anything! It just—"

"You are *divine!*" the man gasps. "Alan, you melted the Rain without praying. Only the divine can do that!"

He drops the bag and falls to his knees in front of me. "Could it be that you are Kalono in the flesh? The God of Rain?"

I gape speechlessly back at him, which he takes as confirmation.

"You are the Creator of this great gift to humanity! You have come to the mortal world to bring great change to it!"

The two women begin to cheer, and my heart sinks.

No matter where I go, I cannot escape that awful name: *Creator.* What will these strangers do once they realize I'm not this "Kalono" person?

How can I shed this awful name that has plagued me all my life?

....

That afternoon, I wander the area around the tent, shielding my eyes from the blazing, nearly unbearable sun. Gazing out toward the distant sand dunes, I wonder what people and places lie beyond.

Edna sits on one of the mats nearby, feeding her baby some bits of fish from our breakfast this morning.

"What's his name?" I ask, approaching quietly so as not to startle them.

Edna looks up at me, squinting. "He doesn't have one. My partner and I hadn't decided before he passed."

"Oh." I shift uncomfortably, trying to change the topic. A passing breeze ruffles the tent flaps again, and I catch sight of some books inside.

Edna notices my intrigue. "I received those as gifts from one of the merchants who trades with my father. He said that books used to be very valuable in the past—that the knowledge they contain is more filling than all the fish in the sea."

I know exactly what she means. I used to read entire encyclopedias on the tablet computers in Terra-Mar, but I've never held a printed book in my hands.

Edna gestures toward the tent opening. "You can look through them if you're careful. The pages are delicate. Don't be too rough with them or they'll fall apart."

Excited, I trot to the tent and kneel down in front of the books, sorting heedfully through them so as not to damage the bindings. The smallest book at the top shows the drawing of a red horse with some sort of spear piercing through its neck. Above are the words, *Catcher in the Rye, by J. D. Salinger.* Cracking open the first few pages, the name Richard Kinsella jumps out at me.

The author of, 'Shoeless Joe,' I remember.

The recollection sends a pang of nostalgia through me. I wonder what Ruben's doing now, down in the vast Scatter settlement. What lessons is he teaching to the future generations of humanity?

I set the first book down and move on to the second one. It feels only slightly heavier, but has many more pages. One single word, *BIBLE,* is emblazoned across the front in gold.

Moving this aside, I proceed on to the largest book at the bottom, the cover showing a man wearing some sort of protective gear leaping out of an aircraft, his arms and legs sprung open amidst an illustrious blue sky. Printed at the top are the words, *The Physical Science, Grades 8-12.*

"Have you read any of these?" I ask Edna.

She wanders over with the baby in her arms. "No, I don't know how to read. Those symbols are just a mess of dashes and dots to me."

As she speaks, I look back down at the last book, carefully flipping it open. The pages are wide and flimsy, some of them nearly tearing from the spine. Turning them slowly, I scan the myriad of pictures, marveling at all the colors that gleam like living, breathing beings. It's so different than the ghostly data that I'm used to.

The book explains various old inventions—automobiles, helicopters, even atomic bombs. One in particular catches my eye—a strange machine with a cylindrical body, two wings of solar panels at its sides, and some sort of pointed dish at the front.

"Satellite," I read the word beneath the picture. "An artificial body that is launched into space for the aid of collecting information and transferring electrical signals between transmitters." Out of habit, I pore over the details of constructing such a machine, trying to understand every last component and function of it.

When I finish reading, I close the book and stack the others back on top of it. "These are very interesting," I say to Edna. "Thank you for letting me look through them."

She regards me silently for a moment, then asks, "Are you really Kalono?"

Caught off-guard, I freeze. How am I supposed to answer this? I've been called the Creator of many things in my lifetime, but this strange thing called "Rain" is something I've never heard of until now. What am I supposed to say to someone who's seen me do something extraordinary with something I know so little about?

"Do I look like the God of Rain to you?" I ask, a wry half-smile on my lips.

She seems to ease, her shoulders relaxing. "No. You just look like a boy. A strange, light-skinned boy."

I smile at her description. It's refreshing to feel ordinary.

I'm no Creator. I'm just a boy.

A boy that came out of the ocean.

CHAPTER 20

These days, I have an abundance of time to reflect on my life. When I'm not sleeping, eating, or drinking Rain from a bowl, I spend my hours pacing back and forth along the shore, staring out at the eternal stretch of water. My submarine is long gone—swept away by the relentless currents. On most mornings, I watch Jarvis and Meckel fling their nets out over the waves, sometimes catching fish, sometimes catching nothing but water.

I sit on the warm sand and dig my toes into it, studying the dismal brown sky. It still looks so strange to me, like the earth flipped itself upside down. After admiring such beautiful images of a celestial blue sky all my life, I almost feel like what I see now is a lie—like any moment my eyes will show me how the sky *really* looks.

I begin to wonder if I'd be happier returning to the Scatter settlement and living out my days with the Builders there after all. But I can't entertain the thought for long.

I'll never go back, I conclude firmly, shaking my head. *Even though the surface isn't what I'd hoped, the truth is better than the lie I used to believe.*

As sea water sprays over my face, my thoughts return to Garrett. My emotions bounce between anger and sympathy whenever I think of him—anger for what he did to my parents, and sympathy for what Ruben did to him.

If Garrett hadn't killed my parents, I could've made it right, I think bitterly, clutching my knees tightly against my chest. *I could've made up for all the time I lost slaving away in that lab.*

I glance over my shoulder at Edna kneeling on the mat, smiling down at her son while Jarvis and Meckel coo at him over her shoulders.

I hate Garrett for what he did. A part of me hopes that he's already gone and dead—his drowned corpse drifting aimlessly through the water, like the corpses of the Neptuan Transporters whose lives he stole.

But another part of me can't forget how awful Ruben was to him. My teacher's prejudice was the reason Garrett even became the Destroyer in the first place.

My mind flashes to that look Garrett gave me just before he left the Scatter settlement to board his vessel. Why didn't he kill me then? All the other Scatters tried to, and he said that he wanted me dead. But he didn't kill me.

Why?

I suspected there was something off about him... Ruben's words echo in my ears. *I wanted to* protect *you from him. If Terra-Mar lost its Creator, there would be nothing to keep the balance of our civilization.*

Balance.

Garrett is the Destroyer, and I am the Creator.

Destruction and Creation... without one, there cannot be the other.

If I had never been born, would Garrett have ever realized his ability?

I begin to wonder about the version of reality I left behind when I first stepped into the time machine. I left that wrinkle of history in search of another. I don't exist there anymore—only Garrett does. Have his destructive ways developed in that time? Has he still destroyed Terra-Mar and Neptua, perhaps to form them into some entirely new place in his own image?

A world without a Creator, where there is only a Destroyer who is also a Recreator... A place where every molecule of every object and being is scattered throughout time and space, then reformed and remolded into something different over and over again.

Would that really be such a horrible place?

Did Garret let me live because he knew that my death would mean his own?

If that's the case, he wasn't showing me mercy, after all, I think, devastated tears now blurring my vision. *He was just trying to keep himself alive.*

Was he ever really my friend?

I clutch my elbows, suddenly shivering as if I'd walked through ice. All the misery that I've been harboring wraps around me, a net of agony and confusion.

I hate Garrett. And I hate myself for being duped. I feel like my anger is consuming me from the inside out, creating a black hole that sucks away at my humanity.

What can I do to be rid of all this bitterness—this anxiety and rage?

I can only forgive him. Only then will all these revolting feelings leave me.

"You hear that, Garrett?" I shout to the ocean. "I forgive you. I forgive you for everything that you did—to me, to my parents, to all the Builders. I forgive you, Garrett. I forgive you, my friend."

The heaviness seems to immediately lift from my chest, like water evaporating from the ocean's surface. I breathe a deep sigh of relief, and push myself up off the sand.

I can only hope that Garrett forgives me, also.

Chapter 21

I tried to create a living being once. I was about ten or eleven years old, when I was still in the throes of figuring out the time machine. Even then I'd anticipated Ruben's expectations, and I wanted him to be proud that I'd achieved what I knew he'd want me to do after creating the time machine.

I created twenty lime seeds composed of various vitamins, minerals, fibers, and lipids, and planted them several inches apart in the clearing on the ground level of Terra-Mar. Every night for six weeks, I returned to that clearing to see if any sprouts had emerged – always scanning the quiet and deserted bridges and platforms above to ensure no one was watching me. But after those six weeks passed, none of the seeds germinated. So, being the haughty and impatient boy that I was, I abandoned the project, and decided to proceed onto something more ambitious...

I was going to create a human baby.

The ground level was deserted the night I resolved to do it. I hid behind the trees across from the lab's elevator, laid one of my sweaters down on the dirt, and aimed my hands expectantly over it. The familiar warming sensation surged through my body as I imagined millions of microscopic cells bonding together, forming the baby's bones and muscles. Soon, a small pouch faded into view on top of the sweater, a little figure curled up within it.

The amniotic sac ruptured gently, the fluid inside soaking through the sweater and into the soil beneath. There, lying on its side, was the baby, his moist pale skin glistening beneath the shafts of light that shined through the platform above. His head was bowed forward in front of his tiny fists, his chubby legs pressed up against his chest in the fetal position.

Life, I thought. *I've just created life!*

A small sound gurgled from his throat as he began to move, and I waited with bated breath for the little thing to start crying. I didn't care if the sound woke the sleeping Terra-Marans above. Their intrigue would only add to the greatness of my achievement.

But then, something strange happened. When the baby opened its wrinkled eyelids, two garish empty orbs stared back at me like bottomless black holes.

What was this thing? This *abomination?*

A dreadful feeling crept up on me. This thing, this *obscenity,* was not what I'd imagined at all. I must have made a mistake when structuring its composition. A human baby was not supposed to look like this.

And then, just as fleetingly as it began to move, it grew limp. Its eyes remained open, though, staring blankly up at me with two endless pools of oblivion.

The terrible feeling expanded within me, filling me with fear and panic. I glanced around the enclosure nervously, as if I'd just broken some sort of universal law and needed to be punished.

That was the moment I realized that I didn't really know how a human being worked. Yes, it lived, breathed, ate, and slept, but there was so much more to life that couldn't be planned or charted. A person's life could not be determined by their genetic composition alone—there were so many other factors influencing it. So many thoughts, lessons, and choices that made up a lifetime.

A living thing had free will. Who was I to assign it a definitive purpose? Objects were easier—hammers for hammering, desalinaters for desalinating. But I couldn't control a living, thinking organism. And that's why I couldn't succeed in creating one.

This thing that appeared in front of me—this *monster*—it was dead. As dead as the iron of the bridges, platforms, and pods above. Dead, like the three obsidian classrooms that I so thought would instill knowledge and integrity upon the students within them. Dead, like the beeping tablet computers within each classroom. And dead, like the fluorescent light bulbs above that shine down on Terra-Mar, tirelessly imitating the life that it supports.

All I was able to create were dead, lifeless objects.

I was no Creator. I was no God.

I was just a stupid little boy who hadn't the faintest clue what he was doing.

Looking guiltily around, I tried to devise a way to hide my devastating folly. When I found none, I bent down to the wet, crimson soil and clawed away at it until I reached the thick roots of the lime tree nearby.

I dragged the little body toward the hole—my hands shaking with each inch that it moved—and let the corpse roll down to the bottom, where it landed with a sickening *thud.* Immediately I flung the sweater on top of it, covering my shame, and piled the dirt over that, patting the spot smooth when the hole was filled.

Standing up, I looked at my still-shaking hands, dirty and tinged with red. I wanted to vomit just knowing that the remnants of that creature were on me, so I ran across the grove of pineapple plants to the old desalinater hidden behind them. Hurriedly I coaxed the water out of its tube, letting the cold rush cleanse me of my mistake. When my hands were clean, I wiped them on my pants and look around once again, suddenly feel exposed and vulnerable

I searched the levels above, expecting to see accusing eyes glaring down at me, even though I knew everyone was fast asleep.

My chest rose and fell with quickened breath, and my heart punched worriedly against my rib cage. I felt so alone, imprisoned inside a huge dead utopia of my own design.

I'd just watched a baby live and die right before my eyes. A baby that I created in my own image—a baby that could've been anyone in Terra-Mar.

I dashed toward the staircase leading to my locale and locked myself inside my pod.

To this day, no one knows what I did.

At least no one human.

CHAPTER 22

I often dream about where Garrett and I would be now if I told him about our future. Would he hate me? Would he be grateful? Would we eventually still be friends?

Before sleep claims me at night, when I'm lying by the fire and gazing up at the infinite stars, I wonder where and when I would give him my message. My thoughts always return to that night when we played catch in the clearing on the ground level. That would be the perfect time to tell him what was to come.

"Me? The Destroyer?" Garrett would ask incredulously as he caught the ball and pitched it back to me. "That's crazy!"

"And you'll kill lots of people," I'd say, snatching the ball out of the air. "You'll assemble all the Scatters and destroy both Terra-Mar and Neptua."

"That can't be right. I've never wanted to hurt anybody, and I doubt that I ever will."

This would put a smile on my face, because the true Garrett was a timid boy with a soft, kind heart.

"Why would Ruben do that, though?" Garrett would question. "Doesn't he know that destroying the lives of people who are different would only cause more destruction, not eliminate it?"

I'd catch the ball and twist my lips uncertainly.

"Some people destroy others because they feel threatened by their uniqueness, not because they're protecting themselves from harm. Ruben was able to harness my abilities for his own benefit, but yours were something he didn't understand. He was in control of my power, but if you destroyed me, he'll lose that power."

We'd grow quiet then, each of us mulling in our own thoughts.

"Well, I think it's awesome that we have so much power," Garrett

would say as he caught my latest pitch. "If we wanted to, we could just leave Terra-Mar and make our own settlement."

I'd nod, because it would be true. Together, we could do anything we wanted—even create a whole new settlement. We wouldn't need anyone to help us understand how things were built, or to build them for us. We'd just create—and if we failed, we'd destroy and recreate again. We'd be perfectly independent and self-sustainable.

But that wasn't the reason we were put on this planet. People needed us.

"We can't just abandon them, though," I'd reason. "They need us to show them that sometimes there will be plenty, and other times there will be scarcity, but through resilience and perseverance, everyone can overcome strife."

We'd play on in silence once more, Garrett with a troubled expression.

"There's nothing wrong with destruction," I'd say to ease his rising insecurities. "People may not understand, but we do. Creation and destruction are just natural cycles of life. What's important is that, through destruction, we become stronger and better than before."

"Or we could just destroy them altogether," Garrett would respond, surprising me with his forthrightness. "If people aren't strong enough to overcome strife and rebuild after destruction, they don't deserve to be alive in the first place."

My shoulders would droop in sympathy. "Forgive them, Garrett. They don't understand us because they have no control over us—over creation and destruction. Forgive them, just like I'll forgive you."

"Well, I guess what will happen will happen," he'd sigh, raising his forest-green eyes to mine. "There will be plenty, and there'll be scarcity. I'm ready for all of that, as long as it doesn't ruin our friendship. After all, that's the best thing that we've created, right? Our friendship?"

I'd grin back at him. "Right. And nothing will ever ruin that."

CHAPTER 23

On the morning of Jarvis' and his family's next pilgrimage to Boreala, I tell them to begin without me, and I'll follow them later. After watching them disappear behind the distant dunes, I turn to face the ever crashing sea and kneel in the sand. I hold my hands out in front of me, close my eyes, and summon the familiar warming sensation as I imagine two sleek solar panels.

When I open my eyes, there is a folded satellite standing in front of me atop a concrete platform, gleaming proudly in the dim morning light.

Reaching forward, I hook my index finger into a small hole at the satellite's center and swing open the door to reveal a small video recorder—its lens poised right at my face. It's wrapped tightly to the walls within layers of protective yellow sheets and surrounded by a nest of wires.

I press a button at the top of the recorder and a tiny green light blinks next to the lens.

What should I say? There have been so many thoughts on my mind lately—rage that I need to release, stories of the Terra-Marans that I need to share, and most of all, questions that I need answered. But now that I finally have an opportunity to voice them, they all escape me.

Who am I addressing, anyway? What's up there, in the vast endless vacuum of outer space?

Stanley and his parents, I think fleetingly, glancing at the all-encompassing blanket of muddy brown. *They're still up there, floating among the debris of their colony.*

I clear my throat, and speak in a firm, strong tone.

"Humanity is alive on Earth," I say, staring straight into the lens. "We fell from the stars, but we're still thriving here on this forgotten planet. Whoever you are, know that somewhere beneath you, humanity is surviving in forests, swamps, caves, and deserts—in the ice and snow, and even in the deep, dark ocean. We've lived here for centuries, and prospered even though the earth has changed—even though *we* have changed. We have proven that we will always live on, no matter what hardships stand in our way. Because destruction isn't the end. It's happened before, it's happening now, and it will happen again in the future. Humanity will always continue to thrive."

I pause to take a deep breath, then look straight ahead, into the soul of whoever or whatever might one day watch this recording.

"Destruction isn't the end."

My throat tightening with the onset of tears, I lean forward and switch off the camera. When the tiny green light disappears, I stand back up and trot off toward the distant dunes.

I'm panting by the time I reach the top of them, and I turn around to gaze at my creation, now reduced to the size of a mere seashell. The sky above has brightened to a tan hue, speckled with the flapping wings of returning seagulls.

Gathering my strength once more, I aim my palms at the satellite, and watch as the folded machine rises atop another cylindrical structure—this one many times bigger than it, and propped above a quartet of thrusters from which fire will burst.

This rocket will be my last creation. From this day forward, I will never feel the familiar warming sensation coursing through my body again, and that will be just fine.

Flames and smoke roll out from beneath the rocket, sending the sand in the surrounding area sweeping away like the receding waves of the ocean. Soon, the projectile launches away.

I watch as my last creation flies up toward the heavens, the sun now bathing it in a celestial glow. Falling down onto my knees, I'm overwhelmed by an awesome feeling that dissolves all my burdens. All my doubts, fears, agony, and guilt rise up with the rocket, accelerating past Earth's atmosphere and vanishing into the endless wonder of space.

Somewhere above, I hope that some almighty being—maybe even the one who created life on this planet—will receive the message that I embedded in that rocket, and someday come down to tell humanity why it's here. For now, humanity will stay on this lonely place called Earth, searching somewhere above for a purpose to its existence.

Who knows? Maybe that being is searching somewhere beneath for the very same thing.

Discussion Questions

1. What do you think would be the dangers of being someone who has Alan's abilities?
2. How do you feel about Alan's great responsibility to the Terra-Marans? Do you think he alone should bear the brunt of their expectations?
3. What do you think of Ruben's influence on Alan? Do you think he was really helping Alan develop his ability for the good of Terra-Mar? Or for a different purpose?
4. If Alan built a better world, who do you think would actually come to visit it?
5. Ruben said this about the people who destroyed the Mars colony:

   "They should have been rounded up and executed like the criminals they were."

   If you knew something like this would have happened, would you agree with him?

6. If you have the power to go back in time and change a specific event for the better, would you?
7. Do you know someone like Garrett in your life? How do people treat this person? Do you think it's fair or unfair?
8. How does destroying something make a person feel?
9. Was it really Alan's fault that so many people were sent to the Scatter settlement? Is his existence to blame for their misfortune?

   "People are what they are, and they'll never change."

Do you agree?

10. What do the terms of Builders, Scatters, and Neutrals mean to you?
11. In Chapter 10, Gina said this to Alan:

    "*Mind over matter...* That's your people's motto, isn't it? That knowledge is all humanity needs to live? That all you have to do to build something is think really hard about it, and it'll pop into existence? Well, that's not Neptua. We're much more capable of creating because we use our *hands*. We are the *true* Builders of this universe. Not you, Alan. Not you."

    Can you think of some real-life examples where these words resonate?

12. What benefits or shortcomings would there be to repairing or destroying broken objects? What about with broken people?
13. In Chapter 22, Alan said:

    "They need us to show them that sometimes there will be plenty, and other times there will be scarcity, but through resilience and perseverance, everyone can overcome strife."

    Do you agree that, sometimes, destruction is necessary? Why or why not?

14. Do you believe that people who build and people who destroy can get along? Why or why not?
15. From what you've read of Alan's thoughts and actions, do you think he ever intended on going back in time to save the Builders?